THE MONSTER OF BATTLE ISLAND

D0967234

MATT KORVER

CONTENTS

ACKNOWLEDGMENTS

Cover design by Jesse Brady. Find more of Jesse's artwork at jessebradyart.com.

CHAPTER ONE
ANGRY MR. PULAWSKI

"Umbrellas up! Brella, brella, brellas up!"

Oof. Was it seriously 7 a.m. already?

"All my ladies and my fellas! I wanna see your brellas!"

I felt around my nightstand with my eyes closed.

"Get them brellas up! Get them brellas —"

WHACK.

I finally turned off the world's most obnoxious song by whacking my alarm clock's snooze button. I rubbed my eyes, grumbled a bit, then waited for the 7:01 chunk.

CHUNK.

Right on time.

CHUNK. CHUNK. CHUNK!

I rolled over just in time to watch some dope with a hamburger on his head hack through my roof and —

SHING!

— fall directly onto my spike trap. He disappeared in a flash of light.

This has been the new normal for the last two months. Every day at 7 and 11 in the morning, then 5 and 8 at night, costumed goons from all over the world descend on my little island to destroy houses and blow each other up until only one is left standing. Why would they do something like that? Fame? Power? An enormous treasure? No. The winner gets an umbrella. I know. Stupid, right? And if you think that's a stupid prize, you should hear the song that it inspired — "Brellas Up." Some kid wearing a space suit put it on YouTube, and it's been playing non-stop on the radio ever since.

"That sounds horrible," you might be thinking. "Doesn't your island have a government that can stop this sort of thing?" Great question. I'm glad you asked. Our island does have a government run by a real goofball of a mayor. I'd actually love to shove a brella or two up his nose for inviting a weird scientist named Vincenzo del Hugo to use our island for his battle royale experiment.

"Well, fine," you might say. "But he's a mayor, not a dictator, right? Surely someone can stop him." Another excellent question. You're full of them. Someone actually did...

Thud! SSSSSSSSSSSSSSS!

Hang on, a bundle of dynamite just fell through the hole in my roof. I jumped out of bed and threw the dynamite back through the hole.

BOOOOOOM!

After the dynamite exploded in the sky, I took a moment to let my heart rate return to normal. Even though I knew these battle royale weapons couldn't hurt me for real, they never stopped being terrifying. After a few seconds, I marched across the room and threw open the window to yell at my attacker. My bald, old neighbor was standing on my front lawn, shaking his fist at me.

"You're going to have to try harder than that to blow me up, Mr. Pulawski!" I yelled.

Mr. Pulawski pulled a machine gun out from behind his back and started firing at me. I dove to the ground until he ran out of bullets. Then I army-crawled to the hallway, grabbing my school clothes on the way out. Now, where was I? Oh right...

"Wait, new question!" you're probably interrupting. "WHY WAS YOUR ELDERLY NEIGHBOR TRYING TO KILL YOU?!"

That is your third good question. You are a terrific question-asker. You should be a reporter or something. The answer to that question is the same as the answer to your previous question. Mr. Pulawski — a retired weatherman and current caretaker of our community garden — hates me. So does every other person who lives in my neighborhood. You see, I was the one who stopped the battle royale. Then I was the one who brought it back.

Let me explain.

Vincenzo told me and my best friend Jackson that he'd return our island to normal if we could win the battle royale and kill his crazy Raven assassin. Somehow, against all odds, I did that. Then, Vincenzo flipped things on me. He sent me a video of our mailman, Dale, who he'd captured thanks to my carelessness. He told me I'd have to bring back the battle royale or else. Oh, also, I wasn't allowed to say anything to anyone about Dale.

"But then you rescued Dale, right?" you might be asking.

You know what? These questions are getting annoying. That was your last one.

No, I have not technically rescued Dale yet, but that's because it's going to be really hard to do since Vincenzo knows I'm coming, and he probably has lots of traps set up by now, and there's even a rumor about a monster in his lair, and just stop judging me, OK? I agreed to stay silent about Dale and bring back the battle royale, but in exchange, I got Vincenzo to improve some things for island residents. We could now beam back to our houses instead of the battle bus when we died, and we wouldn't get hurt by the purple storm. Do you think that people would be grateful for that?

Well, do you?

(Oh, stop pouting. You're allowed to answer questions, just not ask them.)

No, they were not grateful. Instead, they shot at me every chance they got.

I got dressed on my way downstairs. "Bye, Mom!" I shouted as I hustled through the kitchen.

My mom looked at the clock. "Why are you all rushy?"

I grabbed my bookbag. "Big day today."

"Don't forget your lunch!"

"Got it."

"And that physics project."

"Got that too."

"And your rifle."

"I'm going with the pistol today, Mom."

My mom gave me a skeptical look. "Pete. Honey. You'll never make it to the bus stop."

I rolled my eyes. "I'll be fine."

My mom hugged me when I tried walking past her, then slipped something into my backpack. I turned to see what it was, then rolled my eyes even harder. It was a grenade.

"Mommm," I groaned. "I said I'll be fine!"

"Don't argue with your mother."

I shook my head and walked out the door. Over the last few weeks, I'd had to become an elite warrior just to make it to the bus stop since both battle royale contestants and my neighbors were trying to kill me. I'd actually developed really good aiming skills, so I didn't need a giant rifle, and I certainly didn't need any grenades. It was just embarrassing walking into school loaded down with all this junk.

Pew, pew, pew!

I spun around. A werewolf was firing at me from behind a tree. I pulled out my pistol, dove around the corner, and fired three well-placed shots. The werewolf disappeared in a flash of light.

BANG!

I felt a sting on my left shoulder and turned to see Mr. Carey, the gas station owner, lining up a second shot with his shotgun. I threw up a quick wall before he fired again, then built a ramp and took him out while he was reloading. He disappeared in a flash of light. "Sorry, Mr. Carey!" I called out.

I breathed a sigh of relief and stepped toward the bus stop, but just then my phone buzzed. I pulled it out of my pocket. It was a text from Jackson.

"DON'T GET ON THE BUS," the text said.

My heart started racing. Jackson was the only other person who knew about my deal with Vincenzo. Had he learned something new?

"COME TO MY HOUSE. NOW."

I started jogging toward Jackson's house, but only got three steps before a girl dressed as a pink bunny killed me with a single shot.

CHAPTER TWO
ELMER FUDD

"See?!" my mom said as I marched through the kitchen again.

"It's not my fault. I got distracted by a text."

"Just take the rifle, sweetie."

"I don't need it!"

My mom gave me a look that said, "You definitely need it."

"I DON'T NEED IT!"

"Then at least take a shotgun."

"That's even worse!" I stomped out the door in anger. I guess I probably should have done a little more sneaking and a little less stomping because as soon as I got outside —

BANG!

The bunny blasted me again.

The next time I walked downstairs, my mom simply held out the shotgun. I huffed as I grabbed it and marched to the front door. But just as I reached for the doorknob, I stopped myself. This is what the bunny would be expecting. I turned around and headed for the back of the house. I slowly slid the patio door open, then poked my head out. I looked left, then I looked right. Before I could take a step, however, I heard someone whistle above me. I looked up to see a big, pink bunny with a goofy grin waving from my roof.

Oh no.

BANG!

When I walked downstairs again, the thought hit me that this was just like Bugs Bunny and Elmer Fudd. That just made me madder because it meant that I was Elmer Fudd. As I passed through the kitchen, my mom handed me a sniper rifle. "I'm rooting for you, sweetie."

"I'm not taking that."

My mom cocked an eyebrow and held the gun to her chest. "Then I'll watch your back."

I snatched the rifle from my mom. The last thing I wanted was someone from school seeing my mom covering me from her bedroom window. I'd never hear the end of it. I ducked behind our living room couch, then slowly pulled out the long sniper rifle. I used the scope to scan the neighborhood through the front window. There. Next to Mrs. Donovan's house was a tower that hadn't been there earlier. I grinned. Peeking just above the top of the tower were two pink bunny ears. I cracked my neck, adjusted my aim, and —

SLAM!

I jumped when my mom slammed a door behind me. "Mom!" I complained. "I can't aim if you do that!"

But it wasn't my mom.

BANG!

It was the bunny.

When I came downstairs the next time, my mom was leaning against a rocket launcher. I snatched it from her without a word and stomped out the door.

BANG!

Nice try, bunny. I threw up a wall just before she'd pulled the trigger. Now, it was time to get the high ground. I built a fort at a dizzying speed. One, two, three stories high in an instant. When I finished my final ramp, I aimed at the ground, but the bunny wasn't down there.

CRACK!

Ouch! A bullet hit my shoulder from above. I looked up to see the bunny floating with a gun in one hand and a bunch of balloons in the other. What?! I didn't even know that was possible! I fired two quick shots, which missed the bunny but popped her balloons. On her way back to the ground, she switched to a rocket launcher and fired at my tower.

BOOM!

I jumped onto Mr. Pulawski's roof. That was even more dangerous, however, because as soon as I did —

PEW! PEW! PEW!

Bullets started tearing through the roof from inside Mr. Pulawski's house.

"Hey!" I danced around. "I'm getting off, OK?!"

I slid off the roof, giving up my well-earned high ground. Then, I paused for a second to listen for the bunny.

Shuffle, shuffle, shuffle — CHING!

What a wascally wabbit. If my hunch was right, those sounds meant that she'd just built a spike trap behind Mr. Pulawski's house. Next, I could expect her to sneak around the other side and try to chase me into the trap. Not gonna happen. I grabbed the grenade from my backpack and silently counted down to give the bunny enough time to circle the house. Five, four, three, two, one. I lobbed my grenade, then spun around the corner with my shotgun blasting.

But the bunny wasn't there.

Pew! Pew! Pew!

She'd somehow crept up from the rear and was firing her silenced pistol. I built a quick wall behind me for protection, then started running. But the bunny wasn't done.

BOOM!

She chucked a grenade in front of me, and I swerved to avoid it.

BOOM!

Another grenade on my left.

BOOM!

And another. She kept missing to my left. Almost like she was directing me somewhere. I looked up. My grandma's house? Was she trying to get me to visit my grandma? Then I saw it at the last second — right there on my grandma's front porch was a second spike trap. I leaped over it, rolled through my grandma's front door, and continued running.

"Hi Grandma, bye Grandma!" I yelled as I sprinted through her house and out the back door. Ten steps through my grandma's backyard and one hop of a fence would finally get me to safety at Jackson's house.

BWOW!

I did not even make it one step through my grandma's backyard before getting hit with a boogie bomb. I started helplessly dancing and stumbling over myself, desperate to reach Jackson's house before the bunny caught up. I reached the fence and tried to jump, but the music got to an especially jazzy part at that moment. My left leg flung straight out, which hurtled me upside down over the fence. I fell right on my head and closed my eyes until the dancing stopped. When I reopened my eyes, the bunny girl was grinning two inches from my face.

"AHHHHH!" I screamed.

"Hahahaha!" Bunny Girl doubled over in laughter.

Just then, Jackson walked out his back door. "Oh good," he said. "You met my cousin!"

CHAPTER THREE
MACY FACE

"Wait... Macy Face?!" I asked.

"I just go by Macy now, but yeah," the girl said with a grin as she helped me up.

I remembered Jackson's cousin Macy Face — or I guess just Macy now — as the girl who'd always team up with Jackson to play jokes on me in first grade. I mean, they weren't jokes, really, they were a first grader's idea of jokes. Mostly poking me and running away. I still remember the face Macy would make when she'd try sneaking up on me — her mouth in a little circle and her eyes wide with delight. In fact, she was kind of making that face now. In second grade, Macy had moved away from the island, and I hadn't seen her since. She looked a lot different as a high schooler (thanks in part to the bunny costume), but she still had those same big eyes filled with delight.

"Sorry about that," Macy said. "Just wanted to have some fun with you. For old time's sake."

"Oh no, I knew it was you the whole time," I lied. "I was just going easy on you." I turned to Jackson, my face a little red. "What did you want to show me."

Jackson motioned to Macy. "Her!"

Macy grinned and waved her dumb bunny paw. "Jackson said we're going to rescue the mailman!"

"SHHH!" I hissed and looked around to make sure nobody had heard. "Get inside!" I herded everyone into Jackson's house and slammed the door. Then I turned to Jackson. "Would you stop blabbing to everyone about Dale?!"

"I didn't blab to everyone!"

"You blabbed to her!"

"She's gonna help us rescue him."

I looked at Macy, who wiggled her eyebrows at me. "No, she's…" I turned and lowered my voice so she couldn't hear me. "No, she's not."

"Why? Because she's a girl?"

"What? No! Because we're not ready to just barge into Vincenzo's place yet. She'll get killed!"

"I can hear you, ya know," Macy said.

"We're not gonna barge," Jackson countered. "We're going to sneak through that hole he cut into the mountain for his rocket. Then Macy will take it from there."

I looked at Jackson skeptically.

"Look, you might not be ready, but she is," Jackson said. "She moved back to the island a few weeks ago when she heard about the battle royale thing, and she's been tearing it up ever since! You should see her — she's incredible."

I turned to Macy. "You like this?!"

"It's fun!"

"It's fun to shoot people?"

"Oh, come on. Nobody gets shot for real, and nobody gets hurt. Also," she spread her arms wide, "Costumes!"

Before I could protest further, Jackson's doorbell rang. We all shut up and crept to the door. Jackson slowly looked out the peephole. "It's the mayor," he mouthed.

I rolled my eyes and opened the door.

"Well, if it isn't the legend of Battle Island!" Mayor Parfait greeted.

"Hi," I said dryly. I was still pretty peeved at the mayor for starting this whole Battle Island thing in the first place, then directing all his hate mail to me when I brought it back.

The mayor grinned and tented his fingers. "Are you enjoying our new arrangement?"

"No."

"You requested it if I remember correctly."

"That doesn't mean I like it."

"Well, then you're a very confusing young man."

"I like it!" Macy piped up.

"Oh!" The mayor's face lit up, and he stuck out his hand. "Mayor Parfait!" He shook Macy's ridiculous fuzzy bunny hand. "I see you're a fan of our new currency on Battle Island!"

Macy blushed. "I didn't actually buy this costume. I made it."

"Oh, that's great! Just great!" the mayor gushed. "Can I take your picture for the city's Facebook page?"

"Uh, well, sure, I guess."

The mayor pulled out his phone and snapped a picture of the three of us — Macy grinning and Jackson and I rolling our eyes. "We love sharing how much people love Battle Island," the mayor said as he tapped his phone.

"Was there a reason you wanted to see us?" I asked.

"Uhhhh, yes," the mayor said as he finished typing. Then he remembered the reason, and he got all stern. "Oh, yes! Yes, there was. I understand there's a secret reason you wanted to restart the battle royale."

My heart started racing. Had the mayor found out about Dale? If he had, what would Vincenzo do?

"I understand you two broke into Vincenzo's beautiful cliffside home," the mayor scolded.

"It's a skull," Jackson muttered under his breath.

"It's a feat of engineering!" the mayor shot back. "Also, I'll have you know that I asked Vincenzo about the skull thing, and he said that it's actually supposed to resemble a toaster. Don't you feel ashamed now?"

Jackson rolled his eyes.

"Anyways," the mayor said. "I'm here to instruct you that you are forbidden from entering Mr. del Hugo's beautiful home both now and in the future."

I blinked. So he didn't know about Dale?

"There's been a lot of tomfoolery and dancing in and around this man's house, and he deserves better. To keep people — and especially you two — away, the island has agreed to install strongly worded signs around the mountain. Also, we will patrol with air support to…"

"What about Halloween?" Jackson interrupted.

"Huh?"

"What about Halloween? Are we allowed to visit his house to trick or treat?"

The question clearly caught the mayor off guard. "Uh, well, sure. I suppose Halloween is fine."

"So we're allowed to go to his house every Halloween until the end of time?"

"Well, that seems like a long time..."

"What about Christmas?" Jackson interrupted again.

"No! Why would you need to go to his house on Christmas?"

"If we're Christmas caroling."

"Oh!" The mayor hadn't considered caroling. "I suppose caroling is fine. But only if you don't dance too."

"So every December from now until the end of time."

"I said Christmas, not December!"

"You don't go caroling on Christmas Day!" Jackson said. "Haven't you ever been Christmas caroling before? You go during December."

"I don't think I can allow that."

"So the government is against Christmas now?"

The mayor backed up. He did not want citizens to start thinking of him as anti-Christmas. Elections were coming up. "OK, OK! Only during December, though."

"And Flag Day, obviously."

The mayor shook his head. "I'm going to have to clear all this with Vincenzo."

"Well, you'd better do that before you put up your signs."

The mayor started backing out of the doorway. He'd been rattled, but he was able to pull it together long enough to put on his cheesy politician smile on one more time. "Stay safe out there, citizens! Your community…"

BANG!

The mayor disappeared in a flash of light before he could finish his sentence. A pirate had blasted him with a cannon.

Jackson slammed the door and turned to us with a little grin. "Time to go."

CHAPTER FOUR
DEATH BUNNY

"Did you not hear one word the mayor just said?!" I asked in disbelief.

"Yeah," Jackson replied. "I heard that he's gonna try to stop us with strongly-worded signs."

"Well, then you heard the wrong thing. Because he said Vincenzo doesn't want us snooping around. And if Vincenzo doesn't want us there, then we have a lot worse things to worry about than some signs. Like, have you heard about the monster?"

Jackson squinted at me. "What's wrong with you?"

"What's wrong with you?!" I shot back.

"No, I asked first. Ever since we found out about Dale, you've been making excuses about why we can't rescue him."

"I have not!"

"It's too dangerous. Too late. Too early. Too rainy. Too sunny. Now, there's some monster that may or may not exist. So tell me, when is the perfect time to go?"

Jackson clearly wasn't waiting for an answer, so I didn't give him one.

Jackson shook his head. "You do realize it's our fault he's there in the first place, right? So it's up to us to rescue him."

When I didn't respond, Jackson threw up his hands and gave Macy an exasperated look. She shrugged back at him. Then a realization hit Jackson. "You're scared, aren't you?"

I folded my arms across my chest, more determined than ever to not answer Jackson.

"You're scared that the Raven is back."

Jackson hit a nerve, but I didn't flinch.

"Oh, come on! You killed him once already! What is there to be scared about? Do you think you just got lucky or something?"

Bingo. Jackson nailed it. Even though I'd technically killed the Raven, I knew down deep that I'd just gotten lucky. Of course I wanted to rescue Dale — every day when I woke up to that stupid song, I felt guilty that I hadn't even tried yet. But I was pretty sure going back to Vincenzo's lair meant that I'd have to face the Raven again, and I wasn't ready for that. Not yet.

Jackson could tell that he was on the right track, so he walked behind me, unzipped my backpack, and pulled out the umbrella I'd won by defeating the Raven. "See this?" he asked. "This means that you're better than the Raven. You killed him yourself. No one can take that away from you. You did it once, and you can do it again."

I grabbed the umbrella from Jackson. "Thanks for the pep talk, coach. Are we done here?"

Jackson stood with his mouth open, searching for something to say. Finally, he asked, "So you're really not coming?"

"No."

Jackson snatched the umbrella out of my hand. "Then you don't deserve this."

"Hey!" I tried to grab it back. "You just said no one can take that from me!"

"No one can take away your win. But I can certainly take away your umbrella."

I lunged for the umbrella, but Jackson was too quick. He spun out of the way, then held it out a nearby window. "I'll give it back when…"

THUNK!

A plunger shot out of nowhere and stuck to the umbrella. I looked out the window to see that the plunger was attached to a grappling gun being held by a football player. "HEY!" I yelled.

THWIIIIP!

The football player reeled the umbrella out of Jackson's hands into his own. Then he taunted us by dancing and making an "L" with his fingers.

"THAT'S MINE!" I yelled. But just as I started crawling out the window, I saw a muscley Santa Clause aim a rocket launcher at the football player. "NOOOOO!"

BOOM!

The football player exploded with my umbrella.

I turned to Jackson, fuming mad. He backed up. "Whoa. I did not mean for that to happen."

I pulled my fist back. "I'm not going to mean for this to happen, either."

"Hey!" Macy jumped in front of me, holding out an umbrella. "Take mine, OK?"

I rolled my eyes. "So you won one too, huh? Good job."

"I didn't win one."

"Oh, that makes more sense. I didn't know you could buy them from the store, but I guess if you have enough V-bucks…"

"No, I meant I didn't win only one," Macy interrupted. "I've won a bunch."

Jackson grinned at me. "Guess what 'a bunch' means."

Macy looked down. "I wasn't trying to brag. I just felt bad about your umbrella, and…"

"Thirty-seven," Jackson interrupted.

I folded my arms across my chest. Was I impressed? Oh yeah. Super impressed. That was a ridiculous number of victories. But if I acted like I was impressed, Jackson would win, and I would rather die than let Jackson win this little battle.

"Thirty-seven in two weeks," Jackson continued. "They call her the Death Bunny."

I did a sarcastic bow. "I'm humbled to be in the presence of the Death Bunny."

Macy looked a little annoyed. "I told you I wasn't bragging!"

"Fine, you were trying to impress me."

"I was trying to be nice! Get over yourself. I know it's scary…"

"I'm not scared!"

"Oh, really?" Macy gave a little half-grin that annoyed me so much.

"Yeah. Really. Why would I be scared?"

Macy shrugged. "Prove it, then. Come with us."

"Fine!"

And just like that, I'd won my battle with Jackson, but lost the war.

"Really?" Macy asked.

"He's not gonna do it," Jackson snickered.

I gave Jackson a disgusted look. "You're the one who's scared, not me."

Jackson just looked confused. "What are you..."

"Rooooaaaaaar!"

Jackson got interrupted by a terrifying far-off sound.

"Rooooaaaaar!"

This time, the sound echoed loud enough for half the island to hear. We all stuck our heads out the window.

"ROOOOOOAAAAAAR!"

There was no mistaking where the sound was coming from. Vincenzo's mountain lair.

CHAPTER FIVE
THE MONSTER

Here it was. A gift-wrapped excuse to back out. After 65 non-monster days in a row, no one in their right mind would start their rescue mission the second a monster started roaring. I could just say something like, "Wow guys, I really wanted to go, but clearly we can't because we're not equipped to deal with something that sounds like a dinosaur gorilla." Instead, I opened my big, stupid mouth and said in a sarcastic, sing-songy tone, "Who's scared now?"

"Not me," Macy and Jackson both said, even though they were both clearly terrified.

"Well good, cuz I'm not either," I replied like an idiot. And with that, we were off on our expedition. We crept out of Jackson's front door and snuck through the neighborhood. We continued in silence for several more minutes until Macy whipped out a pistol and fired it a few inches from my nose.

PEW! PEW!

I jumped, then turned where the pistol was pointed just in time to see a guy dressed in a llama costume disappear in a flash of light. Before I had time to process that — *PEW! PEW!* — Macy spun and dropped someone dressed in Christmas PJs.

In fact, Macy had plenty of opportunities to show off her Death Bunny skills on our way to the mountain. Instead of scaring people away, the roaring had actually attracted a bunch of battle royale warriors to Vincenzo's mountain. These dummies didn't know what was waiting for them — they just wanted to catch a glimpse of something cool. Unfortunately for them, they never got their glimpse because the Death Bunny was on the loose.

PEW! BANG! BOOM! BAM!

Jackson and I stared in awe as Macy eliminated enemies before we'd even see them. Finally, I had time to sneak in a question. "So, are you like in the Special Forces or something?"

Macy gave me a weird look. "I'm 15."

"I didn't know if they had like the Junior SEALs or something."

BAM BAM!

Macy raised her rifle and fired two no-look shots up the mountain. "I was in the Junior Porpoises in third grade, but that was a swim team."

"Well, then, like how…" I wanted to ask Macy how she got so good, but that would be admitting that she was good — perhaps better than me — which would probably mean that Jackson had won the argument. I wasn't sure if Jackson was still keeping score, but I wasn't willing to take that chance.

"How did I get so good?" Macy finished my sentence. "I live in Tilted Towers and practice all day, every day."

"Why?"

Just then, a grenade fell at our feet. Jackson and I dove out of the way, but Macy calmly built a little pyramid over it. *BIFF!* It exploded harmlessly, then Macy eliminated the grenade's thrower — a guy in a candy costume — before he could reach into his bag and grab another. "It feels good to be good at something."

Hard to argue with that. I was the best at finding tokens underneath arcade machines, and it did feel great.

By the time we started building our ramp up the mountain, I was actually beginning to feel pretty good. Most of our challengers had fallen away, and Macy was clearly the best player in this game — maybe even better than the Raven. That confidence felt nice while it lasted. Unfortunately, it lasted just until the moment we reached the top of the mountain.

"ROOOOAAAAAR!"

We all looked at each other in shock. Even Macy seemed a tiny bit scared. Before I could stop myself, I blurted, "I can stay back."

"Oh, no you don't," Jackson said. "You're not going to chicken out while we…"

But Macy stopped him. Maybe she saw the panic on my face. "Actually, it's probably a good idea to have someone stay outside and watch our backs."

I nodded violently, happy to take the life raft Macy was throwing me. "Yeah, I'll stop people from following you guys down there."

Jackson rolled his eyes, but Macy nodded. "That's a really smart idea," she said. "Do you have a weapon?"

I pulled out the silenced pistol I'd been carrying all day. Macy looked at the pistol skeptically, opened her mouth (probably to say something hurtful about my aiming skills), thought better of it, and handed me a rocket launcher. I accepted it without argument. "We good?" Macy asked.

"Yeah, *he's* good," Jackson mocked before walking to the rocket hole, giving me one last disgusted look, then dropping inside.

Macy was a little more compassionate. "We'll be back soon. Promise." With that, she followed Jackson down the hole.

And then there was silence. Complete silence. It was so silent that I felt like I was wearing earmuffs. I looked down to see if anyone was trying to climb our ramps. Of course, nobody was — the Death Bunny had taken care of all of them. I suddenly felt exposed standing on the mountain all by myself, so I did something I'm not proud of. I ducked behind a bush.

I stayed like that for a while picking leaves out of my nose and feeling a little less scared but much more disgusted with myself. Finally, the disgust won out, and I decided that I had to help my friends. I walked to the hole and looked down to see if there was anything I could do.

I should have stayed in the bush.

"ROOOOOOAAAAAAAR!"

The sound was louder than ever. So loud that the air itself seemed to vibrate. So loud that I lost my footing and dropped my rocket launcher.

So loud that there was no way it could have come from inside the hole.

I made that final realization a second too late. When I turned around, a pair of glowing, green eyes were just inches from mine. Those eyes were part of a yellow face that looked like a contender for ugliest jack-o-lantern of all time. And then the monster's body — sheesh. The 10-foot-tall monster had a big ol' potbelly, tree trunk arms, and toothpick legs, almost like someone had slapped together body parts from three completely different creatures. The monster roared once more in my ear, then raised one of its tree trunk arms and flexed. Sharp claws popped out of its hand.

You'd think I would scream at this point. I did not. I gasped. You see, when the monster raised his arm, he revealed the only piece of clothing he was wearing — a tattered, blue sleeve on his left arm. The sleeve had a patch near the shoulder. It was the patch for the postal service.

Then, the monster swiped.

CHAPTER SIX
VALLEY OF BURNING FARTS

The monster swung so hard that he not only knocked me unconscious, but he also knocked me off the mountain. I spun and tumbled for a long time waiting for impact to come. Then, suddenly, nothing. No impact. Just darkness.

"Hello?" I called. My voice sounded small, so I shouted louder. "Jackson? Macy? Mr. Monster?!"

Then I noticed the smell. It was almost like — and this is seriously the best way to describe it — someone had lit a fart on fire. I covered my nose with one arm and used the other to feel my way out of the dark. The darkness seemed to swirl around my hand when I moved it. Wait, was this smoke? I crouched low and followed a faint path up a hill while trying not to breathe too many burning farts. Eventually, I was able to poke my head above the haze. What I saw took my breath away.

The whole world was on fire.

The purple storm I'd gotten used to over the last few months now appeared to be a magma tidal wave stretching all the way to the sky. Everything around me was either burnt or burning.

I didn't know how the monster had brought me here, but I knew I had to get out. I also knew I had to head east. I couldn't explain why; I just felt drawn toward that direction. I started walking, then jogging, then running as hard as I could. The smoke stung my lungs, but that just made me run faster. I hacked and wheezed and stumbled my way to the edge of a canyon, and then I saw it way off in the distance.

A house.

The haze seemed to swallow everything in front of me — everything except for an ordinary home that appeared to glow purple. I had to get there. It felt like life or death. It was so important that I didn't consider looking for a bridge. I just found part of the cliff that looked a little less steep and leaped. I tumbled and rolled, then crumpled in a heap next to the river that runs through the middle of our island.

Like everything else around here, the river was on fire. I approached it to see if I could tip-toe my way across or something, but there was no way. It bubbled like magma. I searched frantically for some way across the fire, and then I saw it. To my right, a pile of tires had been stacked next to a vine tree. I ran over, grabbed one of the vines, and took two practice bounces on the tire pile before leaping. It worked! I had to pull up my butt to keep from getting burned by the river, but the vine was just long enough to swing me to the other shore.

As soon as I hit the ground, I started running again. The cliff in front of me was my last obstacle before the house. I grabbed a branch growing out of the side of the cliff to pull myself up, then — *OOF!* Something latched onto my arm and yanked me to the ground.

"GRRRRRRR."

I looked up to see two glowing, green eyes. These eyes belonged to a skinny monster with gross fingernail claws. No way I was going to take any more monster nonsense without fighting back. Fortunately, I'd held onto the branch I was using to climb, so I swung with all my might.

CRACK!

I scored a direct hit on the monster's stomach, and it reeled backward. Before I could turn back to the cliff, though, I got tackled by a second monster. This one had patches of fur hanging off its body. I started to take another swing, but this monster yanked the stick out of my hand and pinned me to the ground. I struggled for a bit, then started screaming when Monster #1 returned with a bucket of boiling lava.

SPLASH!

"AHHHHHH!" I screamed until I realized that my face wasn't boiling. The lava wasn't even hot. It was wet.

"Pete!" I heard. "Pete, wake up!"

I stopped struggling and opened my eyes. Macy had my arms pinned. Water dripped from the bucket Pete held over my face. I was back in my room. Everything had been absolutely destroyed.

CHAPTER SEVEN
ZOMBIE RULES

"You sure you're OK?" Macy asked for the seventh time.

This time, I didn't even look up from the bookshelf I was trying to put back together. "I told you, it was just a dream."

"Dreams don't make your eyes glow," Jackson pointed out.

"My eyes weren't glowing."

"Hate to break it to ya champ, but they sure were," Jackson said. "Like neon or something."

"They weren't glowing!"

Macy and Jackson gave each other a look and quietly went back to work. I kept denying the glowing eyes because that's the thing that freaked me out the most. I could explain away the trashed room with sleepwalking. I'd had a dream about jumping on tires and swinging on a vine, so I jumped on my bed and swung on my ceiling fan. Not that weird. People sleepwalk, right? But I'd only ever met one creature with glowing eyes. And I didn't want to consider what that might mean for me. The silence was making me uncomfortable, so I changed the subject. "You never told me what you found at Vincenzo's place."

Jackson shrugged. "We didn't get to stay long, cuz, uh, you know..." he didn't want to bring the monster thing back up, so Macy continued the story.

"It looked like he hadn't lived there for a while," she said. "There were cobwebs and stuff. Plus, the place was pretty trashed."

I looked around the room uneasily. This place was pretty trashed, too. "Did you, uh, find anything else?"

"Yeah," Jackson said. Macy gave him a look like she didn't want him to say anything, but he spilled the beans anyway. "The monster got Dale."

"We don't know that!" Macy said.

"Well, the hospital bed was twisted like a pretzel, and there were claw marks all over the place."

"But no blood, right?" I asked.

"Of course there was blood," Jackson said.

"No, there wasn't," Macy corrected.

"We just didn't see it cuz it was old."

"Blood doesn't turn invisible when it's old," Macy said.

Jackson huffed. "Whatever! I guess I didn't have time to do my crime scene investigation because someone decided to get attacked by a monster."

"Jackson!" Macy scolded.

"There was no blood because Dale never got attacked," I said. That got Macy and Jackson's attention. I took a breath, then dropped my bombshell. "Dale is the monster."

Macy's eyes got wide. Jackson just said, "Noooooooooo."

I told them about the monster's post office sleeve. "Well, maybe he stole it and put it on his arm. Like a trophy or something," Jackson suggested.

"There was something else too," I said. I grimaced as I said the next sentence because I didn't want to believe it. "His eyes were glowing."

"Oh, come on," Jackson said. "You're saying that Dale got turned into a monster and since he attacked you, you're — what — turning into a monster too? Is that it? That's ridiculous!"

"Why is that ridiculous?" I asked. "That's how zombies work."

"I don't watch zombie stuff."

"Fine, but you know the zombie rules. If you get bitten by a zombie, you turn into a zombie."

"Well, guess what? This was a monster, not a zombie. What do you have to say now, smart guy?"

"What I have to say is my EYES WERE GLOWING!" I looked to Macy for help. She seemed to be deep in thought.

"I think we need to get a good look at this monster," she finally said.

"Oh, great idea," Jackson replied. "What are we gonna do, ask him to stand still?"

"We trap him," Macy answered, like trapping monsters is something she often does in her spare time. "I can build a trap. We just need bait."

"Not it," Jackson immediately said.

"Not it," Macy followed.

"No way! You guys can't do this to me again!" I yelled. Before I could start a long rant, I got saved by my doorbell.

DING DONG!

We paused our conversation and went downstairs.

"Good. You're all here," the mayor said as soon as I opened the door. "I've come to let you know that Flag Day is definitely out of the question."

"Oh!" I glanced back at Macy and Jackson. They were both smirking, which meant that they were thinking the same thing I was. I smiled at the mayor. "We were just talking about you!"

CHAPTER EIGHT
BAIT

Let me say this up front: you should not use your mayor as bait for a monster trap. That is not a nice thing to do to anyone, let alone an elected official. I feel like I need to say that first because this next part is going to sound like so much fun that you'll want to do it. Please don't. (Although, to be clear, it was super-duper fun.)

"You're all very kind to help with my signs," Mayor Parfait said.

"Anything for you, Mayor!" Jackson sang as he pushed a shopping cart full of signs.

I planted one of the mayor's "No Dancing" signs at the foot of the mountain. "This should definitely take care of the problem."

The mayor looked incredibly proud of himself. "I made them myself!"

"Noooooo!" Jackson gushed in pretend amazement. Then, he pointed up the mountain. "Can we put them up there now?"

"Shouldn't we wait for your bunny friend?" the mayor asked. "She's been gone for a while."

"She'll be fine. Plus, we have you to protect us."

The mayor was now grinning so hard that his face looked like a cartoon. "I won't let you boys down."

I giggled. This could not be going better. But then we started climbing the mountain, and I began having second thoughts. The higher we climbed, the shakier my confidence got. Would I still be able to follow through with the plan once I saw the monster again? I started thinking about those glowing eyes, and my legs got a little wobbly. Then, I heard something that made my legs a lot wobbly.

"ROOOOAAAAAAAR!"

I glanced nervously at Jackson and the mayor. The mayor seemed to be unaffected by the noise. Jackson looked downright giddy. "Oops, that was my stomach!" Jackson said in an attempt to find out just how gullible the mayor was. "Guess I shouldn't have eaten that burrito!"

The mayor gave Jackson a sideways glance. "That's not your stomach."

Jackson shrugged at me as if to say, "Guess he's not as dumb as he seems," but mid-shrug, the mayor continued his sentence, confirming that he's exactly as dumb as he seems.

"It's Vincenzo's dog," the mayor stated matter-of-factly.

Jackson tried to stifle a laugh. "Oh, wow! I hope we get to see this dog."

The mayor glared at Jackson. "Don't even think about it, buster."

When we reached the mountain peak, the mayor put his hands on his knees to rest, while Jackson and I pretended to pound signs into the ground. After a few minutes with no monster appearance, Jackson began stomping his feet to coax the creature out of hiding.

Mayor Parfait glanced at him suspiciously. "What are you doing?"

"Uh, knocking the dirt off my shoes."

The mayor folded his arms across his chest. "And why exactly do you need to knock the dirt off your shoes?"

"I like these shoes. I want to keep them fresh."

"Oh yeah?" The mayor got in Jackson's face like he thought it was something a tough guy might do. "The only time I knock dirt off my shoes is when I'm about to walk into someone's house. You're not thinking about walking into someone's house, are you?"

"No, sir," Jackson said, stomping harder now.

"Then stop stomping!"

Jackson started jumping.

"And no jumping!"

"I'M HOPPING! NOT JUMPING!" Jackson started shouting all his words.

"THEN NO HOPPING!" The mayor matched Jackson's volume.

"IS THERE A LAW AGAINST JUMPING? THE SIGNS JUST SAY NO DANCING!" Jackson held up a sign for the mayor to see.

"THE LAW IS THAT YOU MUST OBEY YOUR MAYOR, AND YOUR MAYOR SAYS..."

"ROOOOOOAAAAR!"

Finally.

At that moment, the monster leaped over a ridge behind Mayor Parfait. We sprang into action. I laid down a launch pad, while Jackson swung his sign with all his might.

WHACK!

He sent the mayor tumbling into the shopping cart. Jackson then ran toward me. "GO! GO! GO!"

He didn't have to tell me twice, I jumped off the launchpad and deployed my glider. One second later, Jackson did the same. The monster briefly considered chasing us, but the tubby, squealing man rocketing down the hill in a shopping cart was too juicy to pass up. The mayor's cart rattled and bounced as it picked up speed, and the monster nearly tripped over itself a few times chasing it. Finally, near the bottom of the mountain, the mayor hit a ramp that Macy had secretly built and went flying into the air. His screaming shopping cart routine did not go unnoticed by the battle royale contestants. As soon as he launched into the air, someone shot him with a bazooka. He exploded like a glorious firework.

The monster was not so lucky.

Macy had built her ramp out of wood, which meant that it was sturdy enough to hold the mayor, but not quite strong enough to support a two-ton monster. When the monster tried following the mayor off the ramp, it broke through the flimsy boards and tumbled into the metal box Macy had built underneath. As soon as the monster landed in the box, Macy popped out of hiding to close the trap.

"YES!" Macy pumped her fist.

Jackson smiled at me as we glided down to meet her. "Nothing to it."

I high-fived Macy's bunny paw when I landed. "Nice work."

BANG! BANG! BANG!

I backed up when I heard the monster throw his body against the metal wall. "Is that gonna hold?"

BANG! BANG! BANG!

Macy patted the wall. "It's double-reinforced! Nothing's getting through here."

BOOF!

At that moment, a giant, yellow monster hand broke through the metal and grabbed Macy. Macy's eyes got super-duper wide for half a second, then she got sucked through the wall.

CHAPTER NINE
DALE

For a second, I thought that image of Macy's wide eyes was the last I'd ever see of her. But then I realized that Macy hadn't actually gone through the wall. Her bunny costume had. The monster had pulled so hard and so fast that he'd yanked Macy's costume off her body and into the hole. Macy herself lay dazed against the metal wall in normal clothes.

"Get away from there!" Jackson pulled his cousin off the ground. He started to run, but Macy stopped him.

"He's not coming," she said.

"Come on!" Jackson pulled harder.

Macy yanked her arm away and turned back toward the cage. "If he wanted us, he would have tried to break the wall again. He's quiet in there." Macy crept closer to the cage and peeked through the hole. Then she turned back with big eyes. "You've gotta see this."

Jackson and I both stepped backward at the same time.

Macy shook her head. "I'm serious! Look!"

After a few more seconds, Jackson and I ventured closer to the hole. I couldn't believe what I saw. The monster sat in the middle of the floor with its eyes closed, legs crossed, and Macy's backpack clutched to its chest. He finally opened his eyes and noticed us staring. I instinctively flinched and started backpedaling.

"It's OK, pal!" Macy said to the monster. "We're not here to hurt you."

The monster sized us up. Macy grabbed my arm and pulled me closer. "This is Pete. Remember Pete?"

"Uh, hi!" I awkwardly waved while trying to back up. "Sorry about that misunderstanding on the mountain earlier."

I didn't know why I was apologizing for the monster killing me and also probably turning me into a monster, but I decided to play this as safe as possible.

The monster didn't respond, so I pushed my luck a little more and tapped my arm. "I like your sleeve."

The monster covered its sleeve.

"It's OK," I said. "We have a friend who wears something like that. His name is Dale."

When I said that name, the monster widened its eyes and jerked like it'd been zapped by electricity. That seemed like a good sign, so I pressed forward. "Are — are you Dale?"

The monster hung its head.

"Hey, Dale, it's OK!" Jackson said. "Pete here is gonna be a monster too!"

I glared at Jackson. Then I looked back at Dale. "I'm sorry we didn't come for you earlier, but we're here to help now."

Dale shook his head and looked up the mountain.

"Vincenzo?" I asked. "Don't worry about him. We'll protect you."

Dale's monster eyes looked skeptical, so I pointed at Macy. "She's actually the one who's going to protect you. She's really good."

Macy waved cheerfully. "I'm Macy! Do you know how we can help?"

Dale started digging through her backpack.

"He's getting a gun!" Jackson yelled.

But instead of a gun, Dale pulled out a map. He spread it on the ground, looked it over for a second, then pointed to a spot with his big, fat finger.

"Where's he pointing?" Jackson craned his neck for a better look. Macy couldn't see either, so she built a door into the side of the cage and walked right in.

"Macy!" Jackson yelped. But Dale didn't lunge. Eventually, Jackson and I decided it was safe to follow her.

"Salty Springs," Macy said when we reached Dale.

"Where's that?" I asked, trying to get a better look.

"Salty Springs!" Macy repeated. "You've lived here your whole life, and you don't know where that is?"

"I'm sorry, I don't keep up with the dumb battle royale names they..." I trailed off when I finally saw where Dale was pointing. "It's the house," I whispered.

"What house?"

"The house that was glowing in my dream! There must be something inside!"

"Then, let's go!" Macy said as she took her backpack from Dale. "I need this, but you can keep the bunny..."

"ROOOAAAAAR!"

For whatever reason, Dale became furious when Macy took the backpack. His eyes flashed, and he lunged at her. Fortunately, Macy managed to roll out of the door just in time. Jackson and I quickly followed.

"Wait!" she said. "You can..."

BANG!

Macy got interrupted by the crack of a far-off sniper rifle. Then, she disappeared in a flash of light.

CHAPTER TEN
EVEL KNIEVEL

CRACK! WHIZ!

Jackson and I scrambled to take cover behind the cage as bullets flew around us. "Got any weapons?!" I shouted.

Jackson shook his head. "Macy had them all! Maybe we can wait for her?"

CHUNK CHUNK CHUNK

I peeked around the wall. "I don't think that's an option." Our sniper friends — two guys in shark costumes — were now building a ramp and closing in on us.

Jackson glanced back at Dale, who was struggling to squeeze through the door of his cage and maul us. "What about him?"

"Gotta let him out."

"WHAT?!"

THUNK! THUNK!

Bullets were now hitting the dirt in front of us. No more time to argue. I turned and opened a hole in Dale's cage.

"ROOOAAAAAR!" As soon as Dale got out, he started sprinting toward the sharks' ramp.

Ratatatatat!

The sharks turned their fire from us to the enormous monster barreling toward them. I felt relief for exactly half a second until I remembered that it was my job to protect Dale. "Shoot us instead!" I yelled at the sharks.

The sharks didn't listen. They wanted whatever prize came from killing this enormous golden monster.

Ratatatatat!

I watched helplessly as they landed shot after shot. Instead of trying to dodge the bullets, Dale just lumbered straight ahead. He was a big monster, but I didn't know how much more of this he could take.

"What's he doing?" Jackson asked.

Dale's plan turned out to be both simple and effective. As soon as he reached the base of the sharks' ramp, he wound up and punched as hard as he could. That single punch destroyed the ramp and sent the sharks tumbling to their death.

"YES!" We jumped out of hiding to join Dale. The big monster was bent over and shaking. Jackson draped one of Dale's big arms over his shoulder. "Come on, we'll get you to that house."

I stopped Jackson. "And how are we going to do that? Anyone who sees us is gonna want a piece of him."

"We can sneak," Jackson said.

I motioned to the enormous monster. "Really?"

"Then we find weapons! There are always some lying around." Jackson scanned the area. No weapons, but something caught his eye. "That's it," he muttered before sprinting toward an overturned semi-truck in the middle of the road.

"Hey, wait!" I ran to catch up. I couldn't imagine what Jackson was thinking. Unless he'd somehow learned how to hotwire a car, he wasn't driving this or any of the other abandoned vehicles on the island.

Jackson crawled on top of the truck's trailer and wiped away some dirt, revealing the "Perfect Potty" logo. "This is one of the trucks from my dad's company!"

"Okayyyyy."

Jackson dug through his pockets and held up a keyring. "He uses universal locks, which means I have the key!"

"Fine, but nobody's driving a truck that's flipped on its side."

Jackson rolled his eyes and pointed at the truck. "Little help, Dale?"

Dale lumbered over, picked up the truck, then dropped it back on its wheels like it was a toy. Jackson grinned a proud little grin at me, then hopped into the driver's seat. "Put him in the back and keep him safe."

"Wait, do you know how to drive this?"

"Sure. It's just like driving a car."

"Do you know how to drive a car?!"

Jackson gave me a look like I was so lame. "I play Mario Kart."

With that reassurance, I joined Dale in the truck's trailer and shut the door. "Don't worry," I told Dale. "We're gonna be OK."

Actually, there was plenty of reason to worry because we were definitely not going to be OK. Jackson started the truck, we lurched forward, then the truck died. He restarted the truck and went through the exact same routine again. Then, on the third try, the engine made a grinding sound. Dale glanced at me with worry in his glowing eyes. I smiled back and silently prayed that Jackson would miraculously gain the ability to drive a massive truck.

Immediately after I finished, God answered my prayer with a big ol' nope.

BANG! BANG! BANG!

A band of warriors ambushed us, causing Jackson to panic and flip the truck. As soon as we flipped, one of our attackers — a guy dressed as a ninja assassin — opened the trailer door. He maybe should have been more ninja-like because as soon as he showed his face, Dale punched it with all his might. The ninja disappeared in a flash and dropped all his weapons. I rolled out of the back of the truck, grabbed his shotgun, and fired at the rest of his team all in one motion like I was in an action movie. I missed. I took cover and fired a few more times. I missed those shots too. The team quickly built a fort and climbed to the top so they could rain bullets down on us.

Dale finally decided he'd had enough. He calmly walked out of the truck, picked up an enormous boulder, and chucked it at the fort. The fort shattered, and all three remaining members of the team disappeared in flashes of light. Dale calmly returned to the truck, flipped it back onto its wheels, and climbed back in.

I collected our attackers' weapons, scrambled on top of the trailer, and shouted at a stunned Jackson, "Start driving! I'll take care of anyone else who shows up!"

That turned out to be a tough promise to keep because word quickly spread around the island that a new vehicle had just become available, and it was currently being driven at grandma speed by a real noob.

PEW PEW!

I spun around and took out a Red Riding Hood behind us.

BANG!

I had to think fast to kill the bush sneaking up on our right.

CRACK!

I quickly switched to a sniper rifle and eliminated the duo firing at us from the hills outside Tilted Towers.

By concentrating really hard, I was able to take out all the threats before they could land a single shot. I felt great about myself. Then I saw the bridge.

We'd arrived at the river I'd crossed via rope swing in my dream. In real life, there was only one way to cross the river, and it was the bridge in front of us. Unfortunately, every remaining fighter knew that too, and they'd all gathered in the center of the bridge to get their shot at us.

"Back up!" I screamed.

Beep-beep-beep-beep-CRUNCH

Jackson backed straight into a rock. Of course he did. He was the world's worst driver. Everyone opened fire at once.

Ratatatatat!

Well, we had a good run. At least...

Wait.

I couldn't believe my eyes.

Was that...

Right in the middle of the bridge were five barrels of gasoline. Five! Before that moment, I don't think I'd seen a single real-life gasoline barrel, let alone five placed in such a fortunate spot. I pulled out my rocket launcher and fired one rocket right into the middle of the cluster.

BOOOOOOOOOOOM!

All five barrels exploded, taking out the middle of the bridge and sending all the warriors plummeting to their deaths. Well, all the warriors except one.

CHUNK-CHUNK-CHUNK

One lone Viking scrambled to build a ramp he could use to take us out.

PEW!

Got him.

Jackson leaned out of the window and stared at me with wide eyes. "THAT WAS INCREDIBLE!"

I shrugged like it was nothing, then jumped when I heard a bullet hit the truck. I spun around, and my stomach sank. A gang from Tilted Towers was closing in.

"GUN IT!" I yelled at Jackson. "GO! GO! GO!"

Jackson slammed the gas pedal, and the truck lurched forward. We started gaining momentum toward the half-finished ramp in front of the destroyed bridge.

I crawled forward and clung to the truck's cab in preparation for the Evel Knievel river jump that was about to happen. I closed my eyes. Three. Two. One.

Weightless.

I didn't open my eyes the entire time we were flying over the river. Either we'd keep falling until we'd die, or...

CLUNK!

We'd reach the other side! I re-opened my eyes to see that actually, just the front of the truck had reached the other side. The trailer was dangling off the edge of the cliff. Jackson poked his head out of the window. "Grab my hand!"

I tried. But as soon as I moved…

CRUUUUUNNNNNCH!

…The truck moved too. We slid back a few yards until a wheel caught the ground and stopped us with a jolt. That jolt jostled something inside the truck. It took me a second to figure out what that something was, but when I did, my eyes got wide.

"DALE!"

Too late. He'd already tumbled out of the truck.

BOOM!

Dale belly-flopped so hard that he splashed water all the way up to the bridge. Then, he disappeared in a flash of light.

CHAPTER ELEVEN
CAUSE/CURE

"Now what?" Jackson asked.

I stared into the water, stunned. I hadn't even considered what would happen if Dale died as a monster. Where was he now? Would he even come back? Dale quickly answered that question himself.

"ROOOOOOOOAAAAR!"

Even though the sound came from Vincenzo's mountain lair halfway across the island, the ground still rumbled a bit with this roar. It was that loud. I looked up at the mountain and found Dale silhouetted against the setting sun. His head was cocked to the side in an unnatural way.

"I don't like this," Jackson said.

Dale roared again and jumped off the mountain.

THUD.

Again, we heard and felt the impact. Then, a few moments of silence. Slowly, we heard Dale approach.

Thud-thud. Thud-thud. Thud-thud.

It sounded like he was galloping. As he got closer, he sped up.

THUD-THUD-THUD-THUD-THUD-THUD

Finally, he came into view. Jackson and I recoiled in horror when we saw him. He was a little taller than the last time we'd seen him, but way fatter. He also had spikes growing out of his body at weird angles and all his limbs seemed to be a little off like they'd been reattached to his body a few inches from where they should be. His eyes were crazed as he glared at us across the destroyed bridge. He had no idea who we were.

"Heh— hey, buddy," Jackson tried. "We'll figure out a way to..."

BANG! BANG!

Just then, a guy with a long beard jumped out of a bush and fired two shotgun rounds at Dale. That may not have been the best choice.

"ROOOOAAAAAAR!"

Dale grabbed the guy, then smacked him again and again against the ground. Beardy mercifully disappeared in a flash of light when Dale stomped on him. After he finished with the guy, Dale turned back to us. We stepped backward.

"Good thing the bridge is gone," I whispered.

But this mutant version of Dale didn't need a bridge. He took two steps backward, charged, then jumped. He easily cleared the chasm and landed right in front of Jackson and me.

"AHHHHHHH!" we screamed together. But Dale wasn't interested in us. He snarled and bounded over a hill.

"Where's he going?" Jackson asked.

I closed my eyes to picture the house. "That way!" We crossed two hills, then followed a road to Salty Springs. When I caught sight of the house, I gasped. It wasn't an on-purpose gasp — it felt like something was sucking the air out of my lungs.

Jackson looked concerned. Then, he looked back at the village and pointed to a house with its front door kicked in. "Is that it?"

CRASH! SLASH! BANG!

Yup. Jackson and I ran up and cautiously poked our heads through the front door. Dale didn't notice us. He was too busy bashing the living room floor over and over with a lamp.

Crack! Crack! CRACK!

The floor broke open, and purple light from the hole lit Dale's face, bringing the monster no small amount of joy. "ROOOAAAAAAR!" Dale ripped up the rest of the floor, then dropped down the hole.

Jackson and I followed Dale through the hole into the secret basement underneath. "Whooooaaaa," we both said when we got down there. We'd just entered a hidden lab, complete with beakers, vials, and one of those big static electricity balls that they have in every science museum. Buttons, keyboards, and screens lined every inch of wall space. Since almost everything was turned off, the only real light came from the purple thing that Dale was holding. The purple thing seemed to have Dale's full attention, so we decided it'd be safe to creep a little closer to get a better look. We almost got close enough to touch the monster before he noticed us.

"GRRRRRRR!"

Dale clutched his treasure closer, turned, and hunched in the corner. When he turned — and maybe this was just my eyes playing tricks on me in the dark — I thought his skin looked a little less yellow.

"Are his spikes shrinking?" Jackson asked.

I didn't answer because I was studying the purple light. It was the same purple glow that I remembered from my dream. And just like my dream, it seemed to be calling to me. What if this was the key to everything? I had to find out what Dale was holding. I laid my hand on the monster's back. "Hey, Dale."

SNARL!

Dale turned to me with his fangs bared. His face was definitely skinnier now, and it looked like a nose was starting to poke out.

I pressed on. "I need to know what you have in your hand. I'm not going to take it. Please."

Dale studied me for a moment. I could tell he recognized me again. He finally parted his hands a little to reveal a stone. It was just a weird glowing rock — maybe a crystal or something — but it suddenly felt like the most important thing in the world. I had to touch it. The feeling was so intense that I reached out my hand before I could stop myself.

"ROOOAAAR!"

Dale quickly closed his hand into a fist and pummeled me across the room.

Jackson ran over. "What's wrong with you?!"

"I-I don't know," I said, rubbing my head. "I had to have it."

"You had to have a rock?"

"It's an important rock. I think it's making him better."

Jackson shook his head. "Stay over here. Got it? Let him have his little rock and try not to get yourself killed."

I turned my attention to the panel of screens and tried to clear my head. Was I losing my mind? The screens didn't do much to distract me from my thoughts. Most of them had been turned off, and the ones that were on showed computer code that I couldn't figure out.

Then I found the journal.

I almost missed it because the room was so dark, but sitting on a ledge underneath one of the screens was a small notebook. I opened it and got interested immediately. On the first page, someone had drawn a crystal like the one Dale was holding. Underneath it, they'd written "CAUSE/CURE" in big letters next to scribbly scientific formulas that used words like "ohms" and "amps" a bunch of times. The next page's headline said **STEP 1: DREAMS**. I almost turned the page (As we all know, nobody wants to hear about someone else's dreams) but one word caught my eye: "Fire." I read the full entry. My heart beat faster with every word I read.

MARCH 27: Subject reports vivid dream full of fire. Describes odor of "burning flatulence."

MARCH 28: Subject reports same dream as last night. This time, he also saw a glowing house.

The dream repeated for a few more entries, then, **STEP 2: NIGHTMARES.**

"Hey, Pete," Jackson said, breaking my concentration. "You hear that?"

"Not now!"

APRIL 3: Subject reports dream world is now populated by monsters.

APRIL 4: Subject refuses to sleep. Afraid for his life.

"I think someone's upstairs," Jackson said.

"I'm busy!" I shot back.

STEP 3: CONFUSION

APRIL 6: Subject is on hour 77 with no sleep. Becoming increasingly deranged.

APRIL 7: Subject slept for 21 minutes and awoke with permanent glowing eyes. Cannot differentiate between reality and dreams. Becoming a danger to himself and others.

"I think there may be security cameras," Jackson said. "Can you try turning those screens on so we can see what's going on?"

I didn't respond, mostly because I don't think I was breathing anymore.

STEP 4: TRANSFORMATION

"Oh, wait, I think this button might do it," Jackson said.

VROOOOOOOOOOOOOOM!

"Uh oh."

I finally looked up. "What did you do?"

Jackson pointed to the electricity ball in the middle of the room. It was sparking now. The hairs on my arm started standing.

"Turn it off!"

Jackson hit the button over and over. "I can't!"

I looked back down at the journal, desperate to finish it. I skipped to the end.

STEP 5: MUTATION

There was no date or sciency-sounding description for this one. Only a smudge of blood and a three-word warning written in all caps: *DO NOT KILL!*

ZAP!

I looked up to see that the static sparks had turned into lightning bolts. One zapped the ceiling. Another zapped a screen, turning it to static. Then, a third hit the purple stone Dale was holding.

POP!

The stone suddenly turned the same neon green as Dale's eyes, which seemed to make the monster angry. Super-duper angry. He gripped the stone so tight that his muscles looked like they were going to bulge out of his arms. Then, he started growing. The spikes returned. His eyes glowed brighter.

At that moment, the electricity ball shot a fourth lightning bolt. This one hit me square in the chest. I flew backward, smashed into a screen, and got knocked unconscious.

CHAPTER TWELVE
BOWSER GODZILLA

My nose started burning. Fire farts.

"Just a dream. Just a dream," I repeated with my eyes closed. When I'd finally convinced myself, I opened my eyes to find out that I was wrong — it wasn't just a dream. It was a nightmare. Two enormous glowing eyes told me I'd reached Step Two.

"BWAHAHAHA."

That wasn't the normal Dale roar I'd gotten used to. It sounded more like Bowser right before he roasts Mario. The green eyes moved closer. I backed up. Then, the eyes rose in the air. Ten feet. Twenty feet. Thirty feet.

"BWAHAHAHA! ROOOOOAAAAAAAR!"

The monster's roar sent flames out of its mouth, lighting up the room so I could finally see what he looked like. It WAS Bowser! Or possibly a bigger, uglier version of Bowser. Maybe Bowser crossed with Godzilla with extra mutant spikes sticking out at weird angles for good measure. The Bowser Godzilla glared at me.

"Don't worry, I'll be out of your hair any minute now," I said. "Just trying to wake up."

The monster shook his fist. When he did, I noticed that the fist glowed green. He was holding the stone.

Obviously, this was a dream. I knew that even then. But that knowledge didn't stop my heart from pounding out of my chest when I saw the stone. I HAD to have it. I didn't know why, and I didn't care. I gritted my teeth and charged at the monster.

POW!

He sent me flying back with his fist. I shook it off and tried again. This time, the monster didn't even bother fighting me. He just turned around, causing his massive spike tail to *THWACK* into me and knock me backward again. I jumped up, more determined than ever to rip that stone out of his hand. Maybe because I was so focused on the stone, I didn't see the next part coming at all.

WHAM!

A green jackal flew out of nowhere and pinned me to the ground. It got right in my face, showed its sharp teeth, and growled. Its breath was so gross that I almost puked. If that wasn't bad enough, a zombie decided to join the fun. It stood over me with a mean smile on its twisted face.

I sighed and stopped struggling. Might as well get this over with. I looked past the jackal so I wouldn't have to watch it take its first bite out of me. That's when I saw that the zombie was armed. It didn't have a normal weapon strapped to its back, of course — this was a nightmare. It was carrying something that looked like a rocket launcher with a poison pumpkin sticking out of it. The zombie had its back turned to me. If I wanted to fight back, this was my chance.

I waited until the jackal reared back to bite me, then I rolled out from underneath it and stole the zombie's weapon.

SHRIIIIEEEEEK!

The jackal recovered quickly and leaped at me with its claws outstretched. I was ready, though.

BOOM!

I fired my new weapon, taking out the jackal mid-leap. It disappeared in a flash of light. The zombie tried to tackle me, but I spun away while reloading my pumpkin launcher at the same time. I kept my eye on the prize — the stone. When I finally reloaded, I aimed at Bowzer-zilla's back and pulled the trigger again.

BOOM!

"ROOOOAAAAAAR!"

That got the monster's attention. He turned around, spraying fire across the room. That got the zombie off my back for a second, allowing me to reload.

BOOM!

Another direct hit! This time, I got the monster's belly. He stumbled backward and roared in pain. One more shot might do it. Unfortunately, I never got my chance to take another shot because the zombie finally caught me. It ripped the pumpkin launcher out of my hand and threw it across the room.

"NO!"

Bowzer-zilla stomped on the weapon, let out one more roar, then lumbered away.

"Get off me!" I screamed at the zombie. "I need it! I need that stone!"

The zombie did not get off me. Instead, it grabbed my face in its bony hands and screeched.

"EEEEEEEEEE!"

It screeched and screeched, so I screamed back.

"AHHHHHHHHH!"

It continued that way for a while. Both our faces got red.

"EEEEEEEEEE!"

"AHHHHHHHHH!"

"EEEEEEEEEE!"

"AHHHHHHHHH!"

"EEEEEEEEET!"

Wait, did it say, "Eet?"

"PEEEEEEEETE!"

That made me stop screaming. Oh no. Of course, this wasn't a zombie. It was Macy. When she saw that I finally recognized her, Macy let go of my face.

I sat up and rubbed my head. Wait, if Macy was the zombie, then... "Where's Jackson?" I asked.

Macy sighed. "You killed him."

CHAPTER THIRTEEN

MONSTER ON THE LOOSE

I started shaking. "I'm already on Step Two," I whispered.

"What's Step..."

"Nightmares!" I interrupted. "I had a dream before, and now I'm having nightmares, and pretty soon I'll get confused, and then..." I stopped and stared at Macy. Wait. Was I confused already? How did she get in the basement? "Are you Macy?"

"Uh... yeah?"

I took a step back. "You weren't here before."

"I knew where you were going, so I caught up with you," she said in that slow way people talk to mental patients.

"OK, I—I just…" I put my head in my hands. "I didn't mean to shoot Jackson."

Macy rubbed my back. "He's fine, OK? You just sent him back to his house." She smiled. "He probably had it coming anyway."

"Dale!" I said. "Dale was the Bowser monster in my dream! I shot him a bunch of times too! Did he die?"

"ROOOOOOOAAAAAAR!"

A ground-shaking roar let me know that Dale was still alive and well outside the house.

"Come on. Let's go help him." Macy built a ramp out of the basement and offered me her hand. I stood shakily, then wobbled up the ramp through the hole Dale had smashed in the ceiling. When I reached the main floor of the house, I saw that Dale had been doing a lot more smashing. It looked like a toddler had thrown a tantrum and torn down his playset. A huge chunk of the house was now completely gone, which allowed us a view outside. And what a view it was.

Night had fallen, the purple storm had closed in, an angry mob of islanders had arrived, and right there in the middle of everything was Dale. He was enormous. I mean, he was enormous before, but now, he was way, way enormouser. He also kept getting struck by lightning. The stone he held over his head seemed to act like a lightning rod. Lightning would strike the rock once, turning it purple, and Dale would start shrinking. Then, one second later, lightning would strike again, the rock would turn green, and Dale would grow twice as fast. Macy and I watched in awe as that happened over and over.

The villagers did not watch in awe. They opened fire on the monster.

I took two steps toward Dale before Macy grabbed my arm. I tried to shake her off. "We've got to help him!" I yelled.

"Not by charging like a crazy person!"

I started feeling more and more panicky. "I'm not crazy! We need the stone!"

Before Macy could answer, a plane swooped in. Now, our island is no stranger to airplanes. A giant plane lands at the depot every morning to bring us mail and avocados. This plane was not like that. It looked like one of those little fighters from World War II. Stranger still, its pilot wasn't even in the cockpit. He was lying on the wing. Strangest of all, the pilot was Mayor Parfait.

Before we could process what we were seeing, the mayor did something so incredibly athletic and daring that I still have a hard time believing it was actually him. He scooted on his big belly to the edge of the wing and dangled his arms down. Then, just as his plane buzzed over Dale, he surprised the monster by plucking the stone out of his hands.

"ROOOOOAAAR!" Dale bellowed.

"NOOOOOOOO!" I screamed. At that moment, animal super-strength surged through my body, and I wrenched my arm out of Macy's hold. I started bounding toward the mayor's plane in crazed rage.

The mayor stood on the wing and held the stone high above his head in victory, oblivious to the mayhem he'd caused. "NEVER FEAR! THE BATTLE ISLAND AIR PATROL IS…"

BAM! BAM! BAM! BOOOOOOOOOM!

We did not get to hear the rest of the mayor's celebration because the Battle Island Air Patrol blew up five seconds into its first mission. Once the battle royale contestants on the other side of the storm caught a glimpse of the new airplane, they immediately shot it down. The mayor, his plane, and the stone all disappeared in a fiery explosion.

Dale did not take that well.

The giant monster threw his head back, roared louder than I'd ever heard him roar, and directed his full fury toward the poor saps who shot the plane.

"ROOOOOAAAR!" *STOMP! STOMP! STOMP!*

He smashed them all. Then, he took one last glance at the islanders, decided they weren't worth his time, and stomped away to carve a path of destruction through the rest of the island.

Just like that, everything was quiet again. For a moment. I stood in the middle of the crowd of islanders as dumbfounded as everyone else until a woman to my right broke the silence. "He's got the eyes!"

I turned. A dozen people gasped. "They're glowing!" one of them said.

I held up my hands. "They're not — I'm not here to hurt anyone."

A man aimed his shotgun at me. I took a step back.

"It's not what you think! I need your help." Three more people pulled out guns. That made me angry. "Hey! Are you even listening to me?!" Every weapon in the crowd suddenly pointed at me. I got so mad that my head felt like it could explode. "I! NEED! HEEEEAAAAAAAAAAAAHHHHHH!" What was that?! I tried again. "AAAAAAAAARRRRRRRGH!"

That was all the agitated crowd needed to hear. Every person started firing their weapons at once.

Kill them all. Something deep inside of me desperately wanted to tear through the crowd with my bare hands. At the same time, the rational part of my brain was screaming for me to run. The rational part won out, and I took off. My monster super-strength powered me across the open field and over a ridge, which offered a brief moment of cover.

VVVROOOOOOOM!

An all-terrain vehicle with a rocket engine strapped to its back suddenly flew over the ridge. I recognized the driver. It was my neighbor, Mr. Pulawski. For an old guy, he really got around. When he saw me, Mr. Pulawski gunned the engine, making it clear that his goal was to turn me into roadkill.

"Wait!" I tried. "Let's be friends!"

WOOOOOOOOSH!

Nope. Mr. Pulawski hit his jet boost and closed the distance between us in an instant. A split second before he could run me over, I built a ramp behind me and ducked. It worked. The ATV flew into the air, spinning wildly out of control. Mr. Pulawski — bless his fragile, old heart — did not let go. That was very impressive, but also very stupid because the ATV flew right into the side of a cliff and exploded. Mr. Pulawski disappeared in a flash of light.

The mob made it to the ridge just in time to see what had happened. They looked at the explosion, looked at me, then screamed.

"It's not my fault!" I yelled.

They shot anyway. They shot so many bullets. Some of them thunked into the ground around me, some whizzed by my head, and some stung my back.

"AHHHHHHHH!" I started to run. I drew on my super strength to run faster and faster. Soon, the bullets stopped, but I didn't let up. I ran all the way across the island until my adrenaline ran out. Finally, I bent over, huffing and puffing in the rainstorm. When I got my breath back, I looked up to see that I'd stopped in front of an abandoned lodge in the middle of the forest. I opened the door, collapsed on the ground, and started sobbing.

CHAPTER FOURTEEN
LONELY LODGE

Stale marshmallows are both better and worse than you'd think. Most people don't know that no matter how old marshmallows get, they still taste like marshmallows. I think that's nice. Also, since they're much harder to chew than fresh marshmallows, you end up chomping on them for a long time. It's like chewing marshmallow-flavored gum. The downside to eating stale marshmallows is that swallowing them is a lot like swallowing gum. Giant lumps of gum. Your belly can handle one or two, but after half a bag, your stomach starts panicking. Then it turns against you.

I had plenty of time to think about stale marshmallows in the lodge. I'd found five bags of marshmallows well past their expiration date in a cabinet, took them to the lumpy couch in the living room, and started popping them in my mouth. I did that for a long time. Hours probably. What else did I have to do? Without the stone, Dale was doomed to roam the island as a mutant monster forever, and I was days away from joining him. So I ate. Because every second I spent eating was another second I didn't have to spend in the valley of burning farts.

KNOCK, KNOCK, KNOCK

I groaned. The last thing I wanted right now was company. Well, if I was going to be a monster anyway, might as well put my skills to good use. I cleared my throat and growled like Dale. At least, kind of like Dale.

"GrrrrrRRRRrrrrrr."

My voice cracked in the middle of the growl. I coughed and tried again.

"Grrrrr…"

Apparently, the growl wasn't scary enough to frighten my visitor because before I could finish my second roar, the door swung open.

"What up," Jackson said as he let himself in.

Macy followed close behind and gasped when she saw me. "You're OK!" She ran and hugged me.

"How did you — were you tracking me?!" I asked.

Jackson plopped onto the couch, popped a marshmallow into his mouth, and pointed at his nose. "You shtink," he said while trying to chew the marshmallow. "I shmelled ya ah mile ahway."

Macy rolled her eyes. "You don't stink. We just checked every building on this side of the island. Why didn't you put up a beacon? We could have found you a lot faster that way."

"I didn't even know I had a beacon," I said.

"I swear you guys haven't even looked at your watches. It's a button that shoots a beam of light into the air wherever you're at. It couldn't be easier."

Just then, Jackson spit out the marshmallow. "How old are these things?!"

"Hey!" Macy grabbed his face. "Focus, OK? He doesn't have much time left."

I felt depressed again. "I don't have any time left. I'm gonna turn into a monster no matter what."

"Oh, I wasn't talking about you," Macy said.

"Oh."

"We're gonna get you better too. I promise. I meant that Dale doesn't have much time left. He's tearing apart the island, and everyone's trying to kill him."

"Sure, but there's nothing we can do about it."

"There's nothing *WE* can do, but maybe there's something *YOU* can do."

"I'm pretty sure there's not."

"Listen," Jackson said. "You monster people can't get enough of that stone, right? Like, it's basically catnip for you."

"I'd prefer it if we didn't call me a 'monster person,' but I guess."

"And you found the stone in your dream even though it was far away, right?"

"Sure. But it's gone now."

"But what if there's another one?" Macy asked.

I suddenly realized where this was headed, and my eyes got wide. "Nonononono, you don't want me to…"

"You have to sleep sometime!"

"Not if I can help it!"

"It's just going to get worse if you don't sleep!"

I shook my head.

Jackson sighed and grabbed a lamp. "I told you. Hold him while I knock him out."

"We're not doing that," Macy said. Then she turned to me. "I know it's scary..."

"I'm not scared!" I shouted. "Stop telling me I'm scared all the time! You don't know what it's like!"

Macy set her backpack on the couch and sat next to it like she was settling in for a real long chat. "Well, I know what it's like to feel scared."

"Yeah, you look real scared when you're out there mowing down enemies."

"Do you know why I'm out here mowing down enemies?!" Macy ended that sentence with a look that said I'd be sorry if I gave a smart-aleck response, so I kept my mouth shut. Macy sighed. "You know that feeling you get in your stomach before you have to talk in front of the class?"

"Like you're gonna puke?"

"Yes! But also like your stomach is trying to squeeze so small that it disappears. And then your hands get super sweaty. And you start doing dumb stuff because your brain feels mushy."

"Uh, yeah, I guess I've felt that before."

"Well, I started feeling like that all the time. And when I had something to actually be scared about like a big test or something, I would totally freeze. One time, I spent a whole hour in the bathroom because I couldn't make myself go to class. It was super embarrassing."

"So what did you do?"

"Well, I tried a bunch of things that didn't work. Then…" Macy paused like she was going to reveal some big secret so I leaned in a little closer. "I talked to my mom."

"Oh." I sat back, disappointed. "Cool."

"See? It's not cool! Or at least it didn't feel cool to me. But that's the best thing I ever did because I finally had someone on my side! Just talking about my feelings helped me feel better, but she also came up with a bunch of great ideas for helping me even more. Like, she thought coming back to the island might be a fun way for me to learn how to deal with stress, and it's totally worked!"

"Cool."

"Cool? That's all I get?"

"Yeah! I'm happy that you learned how to, like, take tests and stuff, but I've got a real problem. I'm going to turn into a monster in three days! A MONSTER!"

Macy's eyes flashed like she wanted to say something super mean, but she stopped herself and took a deep breath. "I'm not saying our problems are the same."

"Then what are you saying?"

"That no matter what your problem is, admitting you're scared and asking for help doesn't make you a baby. It makes you smart."

I opened my mouth to deliver another biting response, but I closed it. I was scared, and I could use help, but I still didn't want to admit that. I finally just decided to communicate those two things by nodding. Macy and Jackson both understood what I meant.

"There ya go!" Macy said. "You can sleep right here on the couch. We'll be here for you the whole time."

"But what if I go crazy and kill you guys?"

"Then, we'll try again."

"I don't think I'm going to be able to sleep."

"I know it's hard to fall asleep when you're trying to, but counting sheep always helps me. You could also try taking deep breaths or relaxing your muscles or..."

"No, it's the marshmallows. I think my stomach's gonna explode."

"Oh."

I lay on the couch and shut my eyes anyway. Even with my marshmallow belly, I found it surprisingly easy to start drifting off. After the stress of the day, just lying down and relaxing felt great. Just before I fell asleep, my stomach did that squeezing thing. I opened my eyes. "I'm scared."

Macy grabbed my hand, and Jackson put his arm on my shoulder. "We're here for you no matter what," Macy said.

"No matter what," Jackson repeated.

With that, I closed my eyes again and fell asleep.

CHAPTER FIFTEEN
THE SECRET STONE

When I made it back to the nightmare world, I kept my eyes closed and tried to settle myself with a few deep breaths (Or as deep as I could without choking on the fumes). *Deep breath.* My stomach clenched. *Deep breath.* My heart pounded louder. *Deep breath.* My head started spinning.

Since the deep breaths seemed to be making things worse instead of better, I finally just opened my eyes. Whoa. So much worse. I discovered that my head wasn't spinning — the room itself was spinning. I grabbed onto the couch to keep myself from falling over. That's when I noticed that the couch was on fire. Actually, the entire lodge was on fire.

"Help!" I yelled.

Nothing. Smoke billowed around me. I started to panic. Weren't Jackson and Macy supposed to be helping? Had they already abandoned me? "HELP!" I repeated.

Just then, four red eyes emerged from the smoke. Oh boy. Ohhhh boy. "These are your friends, these are your friends, these are your friends," I repeated to myself. That message got harder to believe when the eyes got close enough for me to clearly see what the monsters looked like. One was a crusty string bean with tentacle arms and no nose. The other looked like a melting hedgehog with a crooked grin. "Hey guys," I squeaked as I slowly backpedaled. "You're looking a little scary. Can you maybe talk to me? That might help me feel better."

The hedgehog leaped into my chest and screamed, "GaaaaAAAAAAHHHHH!"

I squeezed my eyes closed, and the room tilted even more. *This isn't working!* Just as I was about to turn and run out of the lodge, a tentacle wrapped around my hand. I tried to pull it away, but it held tighter. "Get off me!" I flailed and squirmed. "GET OFF!" I knew I was probably screaming incoherently in the real world, but I didn't care. All I knew was that I had to get away from the monsters.

The monster held calmly onto my arm through all the flailing. Finally, I stopped and looked down. "It's not a tentacle, it's not a tentacle, it's not a tentacle," I repeated to myself. Before my eyes, the tentacle transformed into a hand. Macy's hand. When she saw that I'd settled down a bit, Macy gave an encouraging squeeze. I looked up. Her face still looked like the string bean monster, but it wasn't as scary anymore. Also, the room had stopped tilting, and most of the smoke had cleared.

"Frokrush," the string bean monster said. I squinted at her. She tried again. "Focus."

I took a few deep breaths and felt calmer.

"Good," the Macy monster continued. "See any stones?"

I looked around and shook my head.

"OK, let's go outside." Macy started to lead me, but I stood still. She turned and looked at me with her confused red monster eyes.

I shook my head.

"Okayyyyy, why not?"

I didn't know why not. But something wasn't letting me leave this room. I remained silent and stared.

"How about this? I'll let go, and you start walking in the right direction. Deal?"

"GAAAHHHH!" the hedgehog protested.

Macy let go anyway. As soon as she did, the panic returned, and the room started tilting again. I closed my eyes to concentrate on the pounding of my heart.

DUM-DUM. DUM-DUM.

When I calmed down a little, my feet surprised me by starting to shuffle. I let them do their thing and kept focusing on my heartbeat.

DUM-DUM. DUM-DUM.

I stopped when my legs hit something. Probably the couch. I reached down and wrapped my hand around an object. My heart beat faster.

DUMDUM! DUMDUM! DUMDUM!

This was it! It had to be! I opened my eyes to see that I'd grabbed... Macy's backpack?

The Macy monster put her hand on the backpack. "It's OK. Keep trying."

Instead of giving her the bag, I ripped it away and growled.

The Macy monster put her tentacles up and backed away. "Just relax," she said.

DUMDUMDUMDUMDUMDUM!

I couldn't relax. My heart was pounding out of my chest. I gripped the bag tighter, and before I knew it, I'd ripped it open. Weapons flew everywhere. The Jackson hedgehog dove on a shotgun. Macy dove on a pistol. I dove on... something. The hedgehog popped up and pointed the shotgun at me. "GAAAHHHH!"

I stood up and pointed my own weapon. The hedgehog looked at it, grinned an evil grin, then started cackling. I looked down. I was holding Macy's umbrella.

"ROOOAAAAAAR!"

I don't know why, but Jackson's reaction made me want to kill him. I held the umbrella over my head and prepared to wipe him out with one swipe. Before I could swing, though, the string bean monster jumped in front of Jackson.

"BLARGHK!" she screamed. Then, she took a deep breath and set down her pistol. She turned to the hedgehog. He sighed and put down his shotgun. Then, she motioned to me.

I tried to lay down the umbrella, but I couldn't. Instead, I snapped it in half.

"AHHH—" the monsters started to scream, but stopped when they saw what was inside the umbrella. I looked down and gasped. It was a glowing purple stone.

CHAPTER SIXTEEN
AIR PATROL

As soon as I saw the purple stone, I snapped out of my dream. I touched it with shaky hands, and a soothing wave washed over me.

Macy gasped. "So that's why Dale was so weird around my backpack earlier!"

"That's really one of the stones?!" Jackson asked. "Why would they put it inside an umbrella?"

I didn't care. For the first time since my mountaintop run-in with Dale, my head was finally clear. I continued clutching the stone and enjoying its calming warmth.

Macy reached for the stone, then pulled back. "Can I touch it?"

I tossed it to her. "Have at it! I already feel better!"

Macy turned it over in her hands a few times, then looked up. "We need to get this to Dale right now."

"Yeah, but how?" Jackson asked. "You saw how big he is. He's not gonna let us get near him."

Macy started chewing her fingernail. "What if we could get a plane?"

"Ooh, maybe we could go back in time and ask the mayor not to blow it up!" Jackson mocked.

"But what if there's more than one plane? Didn't the mayor yell something about an air patrol?"

"OK, fine. What if we did get a plane?"

"We just fly over Dale, then throw down the stone with a little parachute."

"Do we have a little parachute?" I asked.

Macy rolled her eyes. "We can make a parachute. I'm more worried about learning how to fly."

"I can fly," Jackson said.

I shot him a look. "No, you can't."

"Oh, really?" Jackson asked sarcastically. "If I can drive a truck, I'm pretty sure I can manage a plane."

"Perfect, you're our pilot," Macy said.

"Wait, that's not how it works! Also, he can't drive a truck!"

nnnNNNNNNNRRRRRROOOOOOOM!

Macy's face lit up, and she pointed to the sky. "There's one now!"

"HE CAN'T FLY A PLANE!" I yelled after her as she and Jackson ran outside. I caught up to them just in time to see the plane fly away.

"HEY!" Macy called after it. "YOU WANT A PIECE OF THIS?!" She fired a few shots at the plane to get its attention. It worked. The pilot turned around and started diving toward us.

"Do we know if the planes have guns?" I asked nervously.

Ratatatatatat!

The pilot answered my question before Macy could. All three of us dove for cover as the plane buzzed right over the lodge.

"What exactly was the goal there?" I asked Macy when the plane had climbed back into the sky.

"I figured we'd think of something."

"I just thought of something," Jackson said as he pulled a plunger grappling gun out of his backpack.

The plane turned around and started flying toward us again.

It took me a second to figure out Jackson's idea, but when I did, I grabbed him. "Are you crazy?!"

Jackson shook me off. "Got any better ideas?"

Before I could rattle off a list of 10,000 better ideas, the plane started shooting again. Macy and I dove out of the way, but Jackson stood firm. "Juuuuuuust a little closer," he muttered.

nnnNNNNNNRRRRROOOOOOOOM!

The pilot must have been new to this whole shooting-while-flying thing because a jillion bullets sprayed the ground, but none actually hit Jackson. The pilot banked left for a third pass, and Jackson shot his plunger right at the plane's belly.

THWAAAAACK!

Direct hit! Jackson grappled up to the plane, swung onto the wing, and took out the pilot with a single shot. Then he climbed into the pilot seat and almost flew straight into the ground trying to land.

NnnnNNNNNRROOOOOOOOOO

"PULL UP! PULL UP!" Macy and I screamed.

Somehow, Jackson avoided crashing. Macy and I used Jackson's grapple move to get ourselves into the plane before he could attempt another landing. I settled into the seat behind Jackson, and Macy stood on the wing like she was some kind of daredevil.

"Let's goooooo!" Jackson whooped as he pulled the plane high into the air. He flew so high, in fact, that the plane started to sputter.

Putt-putt-putt

After the third "putt," the engine died, and we started falling tail-first.

"AHHHHH!" Macy screamed while gripping onto the edge of the wing. Jackson screamed while flipping every switch in the cockpit. I screamed while holding the sides of my face in a classic scream pose.

Jackson finally found the right switch, and the engine kicked back on just in time. "Everything's cool!" Jackson said when he leveled the plane back out. "Won't happen again." He then flipped another switch, which fired a hidden rocket booster and almost sent Macy off the wing.

When Macy finally regained her footing, she marched down the wing and grabbed Jackson's collar. "I'll take it from here."

"I can do it!" Jackson clutched the steering yoke harder.

Instead of arguing with her cousin, Macy hip-checked his head. She hit Jackson with enough force to throw him off balance, but not quite hard enough for him to let go of the steering yoke. It was, unfortunately, exactly hard enough to send us into a barrel roll.

"WHOOAAA!"

Macy held Jackson's shirt, then used the plane's momentum to flip him out of the pilot's chair at the end of our roll. "I said I'll take it from here," she said as she settled in.

"Hmmmph."

I'd had enough of the drama up front. "Guys! We need to find Dale!"

"Found him," Macy said as she pointed up ahead.

I leaned over to peek around her and gasped when I saw the remains of Tilted Towers. Most of the skyscrapers were gone, and the ones that remained had actually started to tilt. Multiple armies were running in with rocket launchers, and several other planes buzzed around the city. And then there was Dale. I gulped. A Godzilla-sized Dale stood right in the middle of all the wreckage beating his chest.

"Jackson! You're up!" Macy yelled.

"Up for what?! We don't have any tiny parachutes!"

"You're gonna have to glide down there and hand him the stone yourself."

Just then, Dale wound up and clobbered a plane out of the sky. "Not sure he's gonna let me do that," Jackson said.

"You gotta try." I handed Jackson the bottom half of my umbrella.

Jackson sighed. "Just get me as close as you can."

Macy nosed the plane down. By this time, Dale had climbed to the top of the clock tower so he could swipe at more planes. "Jump now!" Macy yelled.

Jackson edged toward the tip of the wing. "I come in peace!" he yelled toward Dale. Then, he jumped. "I COOOOOOOOME IIIIIIIIN PEEEEEEEEEAAAAAAAAA..."

Dale grabbed Jackson out of the air before he could finish his sentence. Jackson looked scared, but he knew what he had to do. He held up the glowing stick and attempted a smile. "For you!"

Dale glared at Jackson, glared at the stone, then squeezed. Jackson disappeared in a flash of light.

"NO!" I yelled.

Dale took a second look at the stone, then flicked it at one of the attacking planes. Somebody shot it out of the sky, and it disappeared in a small, purple poof.

CHAPTER SEVENTEEN
INTO THE STORM

Macy and I looked at each other with "what now?" expressions. We only had half an umbrella left, and that apparently wasn't powerful enough to do anything for Dale at his current size. Plus, the storm was closing in, so even if we somehow convinced Dale to hold onto the stone, lightning would likely turn it green and make matters much, much worse.

We silently circled the city as Dale got blasted again and again. Even though he was still roaring and throwing chunks of concrete at his attackers, I could tell that he was losing steam. He stumbled here and there, and his eyes weren't glowing nearly as bright as they had been. In a few minutes, it would all be over.

"I can't watch," I said. "I need to go home."

Macy looked sad. "I wish I could go home." She pointed at one of the few remaining apartment buildings below. It was leaning heavily to the right, and its roof had an enormous hole in it. "When that building goes down, this backpack is the only thing I'll have left. Everything I own is in that apartment."

That made me stop. "Everything?"

Macy sighed. "Pretty much."

"Including your other umbrellas?"

"Well yeah, but…"

"How many do you have again?"

"Thirty-seven. But come on. If Dale doesn't kill me before I get to my apartment, he'll smash the whole thing once I get inside."

"No he won't."

"Oh yeah?" Macy smirked sadly. "Why not?"

"Cuz I'm gonna stop him."

"That's sweet of you, Pete. It's really, really sweet. But…"

"Fly straight."

Macy turned and raised an eyebrow. Something in my voice must have surprised her. Maybe it sounded more confident than she'd expected. It was certainly more confident than I'd expected. "You want to fly into the storm?"

I nodded.

Macy shrugged and hit the boost. "I don't know how these planes do around lightning, so we may need to…" She stopped in the middle of her sentence and turned again. I was holding my half of the umbrella and climbing onto the wing. "Pete! No!"

I steadied myself and held the umbrella over my head. "Jump to your apartment, and don't look back. Get all your umbrellas up to the roof as fast as you can."

"NO!" Macy yanked the steering yoke to turn the plane around.

"When all the umbrellas are up there, put up one of those beacons you were talking about."

Macy almost had the plane turned around when the storm caught up to us.

ZZZZZT!

A bolt of lightning struck my umbrella. The stone inside flashed green, and my hand went numb. That's when I thought maybe this was a bad idea. My whole body started shaking, and my vision got cloudy. "AhhhhhHHHHHHHH!" The stone felt like it was searing my hand. I tried to drop it, but I couldn't. Everything burned and spun, and then, suddenly, it stopped.

My eyes refocused, and I looked down at Macy. Way down. She looked tiny, and she looked terrified. I wanted to murder her.

"Jump!" I yelled. But that's not what came out of my mouth. What I actually said was, "ROOOOAAAAAAAAAR!"

CHAPTER EIGHTEEN
PETE SMASH

Ever wonder why the Incredible Hulk never says much beyond, "HULK SMASH"? I mean, come on, Hulk. All your fighting buddies are chattering away with witty one-liners, and you can't manage more than two words — one of which is your name?!

I'm happy to report that I can now offer insight into the Hulk's vocabulary. When the lightning struck and I turned into a full-fledged monster, I no longer felt confused and scared. I no longer felt much of anything, actually, except for one emotion: anger. Pure hatred for everyone and everything coursed through my body. The only thing I could think was, "PETE SMASH!" and the only thing I could say was, "ROOOOAAAAAR!"

Macy screamed until I swiped at her. Then she jumped.

For a moment, I was alone in the airplane. The lightning struck my umbrella again and again, causing me to grow faster. The plane started to whine and dip. I looked down. The seat that used to hold my whole body was now too small for even one of myyellow feet. Also, I had no way of landing because my hands were way too big for the controls. My crazed monster brain briefly considered jumping, but then —

PUTT-PUTT-PUTT

I became too big for the small aircraft, and it stalled out. The plane started gliding to the ground. By shifting my weight, I was able to surf toward the mayhem at Tilted Towers. As I got closer, I caught sight of Macy gliding toward her apartment building. Dale did too.

"ROOOAAAAAAR!"

He backhanded a plane out of the air and started lumbering toward Macy. I clenched my teeth. All my anger focused on Dale. I crouched lower and leaned forward to dive faster. Dale didn't see me coming.

POW!

I crashed into his head, and we tumbled to the ground.

BOOF!

Dale smashed me with his fist so hard that I flew backward and knocked over a wall. Lying on the ground, I suddenly felt a lot more human than monster. And compared to Dale, I felt very, very small. I wobbled to my feet and tried to find the big monster through the fire and smoke. Turns out, I didn't have to look. Dale found me.

"OOF!"

He emerged from the haze and tackled me. I tried to roll free, but Dale held me down and pummeled me over and over.

PUNCH! PUNCH! PUNCH!

Have you ever been punched by a bus before? It's not fun. I started to black out, and my mind began losing its grip. *The monster on the bus goes punch, punch, punch. Punch, punch, punch. Punch, punch, punch.* Through squinted eyes, I saw Dale wind up for one finishing smash. Then, I caught a glimpse of something else. A tiny figure holding an armful of umbrellas on the building that had tilted over me. Suddenly, I remembered why I was there. My eyes snapped open, and I mustered enough strength to roll my head out of the way.

SMASH!

Dale punched the concrete so hard that his hand got stuck in the ground. He roared in pain, and I wriggled away. Even though Dale was much bigger and stronger than me, I was way faster than him. His extra weight plus the damage he'd already taken from planes and bazookas made him move like one of those big, slow bosses you play at the end of a video game. I just had to let him chase me long enough for Macy to finish her job. Should be pretty simple...

WHIZZ!

...Unless he figured out that he could throw things at me. I ducked just in time to dodge a restaurant sign.

WHOOSH!

That was a car. I dove behind a building for cover. That provided temporary relief from Dale, but not from a brave member of the mayor's Air Patrol.

nnnNNNNRRRRRROOOOOOOOM!
RATATATATATAT!

The bullets felt like someone was throwing gravel at me. I let the plane get close, then snatched it out of the air. I rolled around the building and launched the plane right into Dale's forehead. I threw it hard enough that it just kind of stuck there for a second before Dale smacked it off his face. Then he locked eyes with me again.

"ROOOAAAAR!"

I cracked my neck. My monster brain was done running from this guy. I was ready to fight. "ROOOAAAAAAAAAAAAAAR!" I started sprinting toward Dale. He glared in hatred and lumbered toward me. We met in the middle of the city and jump-punched each other.

What followed was an enormous monster battle that ranged over the whole city. I would describe it, but it's not actually as cool to read about as you'd think. Like, have you ever seen a Transformers movie? Most of the movie is just lame characters talking to each other, but you're like, "It's OK because giant robots are going to start fighting each other soon." And then, finally, the robots start fighting. And you want to be into it. You really do. But it's just a bunch of whirring metal parts crashing into each other. It'd be like if you put a bunch of tools in the dryer and started it up. I mean, it's a little better than that because a Transformer movie won't ruin your dryer, but for those few minutes that the dryer is going, it is almost exactly the same entertainment value as watching robots punch each other. Anyways, if the Transformers robot fights aren't exciting to watch even though they cost tens of millions of dollars to make, can you imagine how boring it would be to *read* a description of the fight?

So here's the short version: I hit Dale pretty hard a bunch of times. Dale hit me very hard a lot more times. We knocked over pretty much every building in the entire city. The only one standing was Macy's. I kept looking back at the apartment for Macy's beacon. Come on, what was taking so long?

BOOF!

Dale caught me off guard and knocked me on my back. That's when I saw it — not Macy's beacon. The first lighting strike.

We were too late. The storm had arrived.

CHAPTER NINETEEN
LIGHTNING

Immediately after the first bolt of lightning struck Tilted Towers, Macy's beacon went up. I tried to roar a warning, but I was too late — Dale saw the beacon too. Even worse, he saw the purple glow coming from all the umbrellas Macy had cracked open. He tossed me aside and raced toward the building.

CRASH! The first lightning bolt hit the roof, turning the stones green.

Dale sped up. That was the moment Macy realized this was going to end poorly.

CRASH! The stones turned purple again.

Macy tried building a fort around the stones, but Dale quickly scaled the building and smashed her puny fort. Then, he reached down with both hands, grabbed a bunch of stones, and held them above his head in victory.

CRASH! CRASH! CRASH!

Lightning began striking Dale's fists over and over. Like before, Dale grew then shrunk, grew then shrunk, always growing more than he shrunk. "HELLLLP!" Macy screamed as she scrambled away.

I was on my way, but not to help. When I saw the purple glow, my monster brain took full control again, and nothing mattered besides grabbing stones for myself. I reached the roof right after the lightning started striking Dale and scooped up an armful of the leftover stones. Holding multiple stones at once seemed to multiply the effect, and I started shrinking really fast. After a few seconds, I could think with my regular brain again, and I wondered why the lightning wasn't hitting me. One glance up at Dale gave me the answer. It looked like some sort of concert up there with a pulsing strobe light. Since Dale was so tall, he was attracting all the lightning. Each bolt of electricity turned his fists a different color.

FLASH! Green. *FLASH!* Purple. *FLASH!* Green. *FLASH!* Purple.

I couldn't bear to keep looking. Here I was

healing myself while Dale died this gruesome death. I had to do something. I turned to Macy. "BACKPACK!"

She tossed me her backpack, and I started tearing through it. Pistol. Hunting rifle. Stink grenades. Nothing that could come close to prying the stones out of Dale's hands. I threw the backpack onto the ground, and a front flap opened to reveal something that Macy had used the very first time I'd met her — a pack of self-inflating balloons.

Wait. That's it.

I ripped open the pack and pulled the tabs on the first two. *THWIP! THWIP!*

"What are you doing?!" Macy asked.

No time to explain. "Just get off this building before it crumbles!" I opened two more balloons. *THWIP! THWIP!* I felt light. Two more should do it. *THWIP! THWIP!* I started floating — slowly at first, then faster and faster. As I rose, I studied the lightning pattern.

FLASH! Purple. *FLASH!* Green.

If this was going to work, I'd need to time it just

right. I held my own purple stones to my chest and hunched over to hide them.

FLASH! Purple. *FLASH!* Green.

Up to Dale's eye level now. Just a few more seconds before I'd get above his fists.

FLASH! Purple. *FLASH!* Green.

And just like that, I was looking down on Dale. I waited until his fists turned purple again...

FLASH!

...And I raised my own fistful of stones.

FLASH!

Now I was the one glowing green. My hand went numb again, and electricity jolted through my body. I felt the monster inside me return, but I refused to let go of either the balloons or the stones. I was worried about one thing and one thing only — Dale. I looked down to search for him. It took a few seconds to see what was going on because my vision had gone blurry, but I finally spotted a purple glow and shrinking monster. I did it.

FLASH! FLASH! FLASH! FLASH!

I held on through lightning bolt after lightning bolt. Pretty soon, the balloons couldn't keep me in the air.

FLASH!

I started dropping quickly. When I looked down to check my landing, I saw Macy leading Dale down a ramp she had built off of the building. One second later, I hit the roof hard.

SMASH!

After that, my vision started getting dark. Lightning struck again and again, and I grew impossibly large. The building finally crumbled under my weight. I vaguely remember a single plane flying at me through the storm. As it got closer, I could see that it held a familiar face. I squinted. No, wait. Two familiar faces. My brain was too far gone to figure out who they were, though. I lazily swiped at them, then passed out.

CHAPTER TWENTY
BRELLAS UP

"Umbrellas up! Brella, brella, brellas up!"

Oh nooooooo. I knew instantly that I did not go to heaven. Because if I did, this song would surely not be playing.

"All my ladies and my fellas! I wanna see your brellas!"

"How do you shut this thing off?!"

My eyes snapped open, and I saw Macy pressing every button on my alarm clock. I was so confused.

"Get them brellas up, get them brellas up!"

Wait a second. I looked at my hands. They were normal! I looked up again to ask what was going on, but before I could open my mouth, Jackson had clubbed my alarm clock with a bat.

"Get them—" FITZ!

Jackson nodded his approval. "I hate that song."

"Did you just smash my alarm clock?!"

"I also saved your life an hour ago. But sure, focus on the alarm clock."

"Is he awake?!" A third figure ran into my room. It was Dale, back in his mailman's outfit like nothing had ever happened.

I was struggling to keep up. "Why are you all here? Is this a dream?!"

Dale swallowed me in a big hug. He smelled like he hadn't showered in a month, which made sense, I guess. "Thank you! Thank you, thank you, thank you!"

When he finally let go, Macy gestured to Jackson. "Now, you owe him a hug."

I sat up. "Seriously. Can someone... Yipes!" I shrunk under my covers when a fourth person entered the room. "Mr. Pulawski! Please don't kill me!"

My elderly neighbor didn't pull out a gun. Instead, he stood over my bed with his arms folded across his chest and harumphed.

"Actually, you owe him a hug, too," Macy said.

"If someone doesn't tell me what's going on right now, I'm gonna lose it!"

Finally, Jackson explained. After Dale had killed him and sent him back to his house, Jackson started racing back to Tilted Towers. But as soon as he left his house, he bumped into the newest member of the Battle Island Air Patrol — Mr. Pulawski. When Jackson discovered that Mr. Pulawski was on his way to battle the great monster, he begged to join him in the plane. "He wasn't going to let me until I told him that he'd get a chance to shoot your plane down too," Jackson said.

"True," Mr. Pulawski confirmed with a little smirk.

Jackson continued his story. Their plane arrived at Tilted Towers at the same time the lightning storm did. Mr. Pulawski was just about to turn around when he saw me transform from a monster back into myself. That sight made him smile and hit his thrusters. He was finally going to get his revenge. Then he saw what I did for Dale and stopped. Jackson said he sat back in silence and watched as I floated above the monster, took the lightning for him, and let him escape. "Then, he turned around and said — well, Mr. Pulawski, tell him what you said!"

"We need to help that boy," Mr. Pulawski said proudly.

"Can you believe it?! I had no idea how to help you, but Mr. Pulawski did. He flew above you, then started pulling wires and metal out of the cockpit. I thought he was going crazy, but — did you know he used to be a weatherman?"

"I think so."

"Anyway, he built a lightning rod super fast. It was incredible! Then, he did the same thing you did for Dale. He waited until you turned purple, then put up the lightning rod. We both jumped, and the plane took the rest of the lightning while you shrunk."

I had a million questions, but I was too stunned to ask any of them. Unfortunately, one final person walked into the room before I could get my mouth to work again.

"Hello!" Mayor Parfait greeted with his big politician smile.

All of us groaned except Dale. "Hi, Mayor!"

"Oh!" the mayor said, clearly surprised to see the island mailman. "Good to see you, Dave! Back from your vacation?"

"Oh, it's Dale, sir. And I wasn't on vacation, I was..."

Jackson interrupted when he saw that the mayor was holding an umbrella. "Drop that! It's dangerous!"

The mayor looked down, confused. "Uh, no. It's just an umbrella. And it's for you!" He held it out to Jackson. All of us jumped back and screamed. The mayor looked more confused than ever. "It's a gift for defeating the monster. I guess you don't have to accept it."

"You don't understand," Macy said. "There's a stone hidden in there that turns people into monsters when it gets zapped by electricity!"

The mayor furrowed his eyebrows at her while he decided if she was serious. He finally laughed. "That's a good one!"

"It's true!"

"Why would Vincenzo want to turn people into monsters?"

"Not just any people," I said. "The best fighters! Only winners of a battle royale get umbrellas!" Everything suddenly clicked into place. "He set up this whole thing so he could find the best fighters in the world and turn them into his monster army!"

"AHAHAHA!" The mayor doubled over in laughter. "You kids and your imaginations." He held the umbrella out to Jackson. "Seriously, take it. If you hurry, you should be able to make the concert."

"What concert?"

"Oh, haven't you heard?! That wonderful astronaut singer is putting on a free concert!"

My blood ran cold. "Not the guy who..."

"Get them brellas up!" the mayor sang like a dad trying to be cool.

Macy pushed past the mayor. "We gotta go!"

We sprinted out the door. "Where did he say the concert was?!"

Dale's eyes widened. "THERE!"

In the field just outside our neighborhood, hundreds — maybe thousands — of people had gathered around a stage. There were flashing lights, fog machines, and loud music. A guy with an astronaut helmet hiding his face walked out to a roar from the crowd.

"WHAT UP BATTLE ISLAANNNNNND?!" the man said. "Everyone got them brellas?!"

On cue, the crowd held up a sea of umbrellas.

"NOOOOOOOO!" our group screamed. Macy ran to a girl in the back and practically tackled her. "PUT IT DOWN!"

A beat started thumping from the speakers. "UMBRELLAS UP!" the man yelled. "Brella, brella, brellas up!" As one, the crowd began pumping their umbrellas in the air with the beat.

I searched the sky. No clouds. Maybe we were just being paranoid?

"What do we do?!" Jackson yelled over the music.

Dale pointed to a tall black object next to the stage. "That generator is powering the stage! If we shut it off, we shut down the concert!"

I nodded to Jackson. "Let's go!"

We started pushing through the crowd, but it was slow going. Meanwhile, the party was just getting started.

"Ladiiiiiieeeees!" the man yelled.

"Woo!" the ladies in the crowd yelled back.

"Felllllaaaaaas!"

"Woo!"

"Get! Them! Brellas!"

BOOM!

On "brellas," a massive sound shook the ground. I stopped and looked up. Had a speaker blown?

No. It was worse than that. Much, much worse.

I grabbed Jackson and pointed to the sky. "LOOK!"

The rocket from Vincenzo's lair had finally launched. The concert paused for a second as everyone stopped to watch the rocket. The singer spread his arms like he was the one responsible for the launch, then pointed up.

KABOOOOOOM!

As soon as the rocket reached the clouds, it blew up in a colorful firework explosion. The crowd roared its approval.

"Get them brellas up! Get them brellas up!" the singer chanted.

"Get them brellas up! Get them brellas up!" the crowd replied.

The explosion wasn't done, though. It spread quickly, causing the sky to do this weird ripple thing. The ripples grew until they turned into massive purple clouds. The crowd was so wrapped up in the song, however, that they didn't notice.

At that moment, the singer turned to me and Jackson. I couldn't see his eyes through the black astronaut helmet, but I could feel them staring directly into mine as he roared the next two words.

"BRELLAS UP!"

Every umbrella in the field went up. Just then, the clouds produced a massive cluster of lightning unlike anything I'd ever seen.

ZAP!

The lightning struck every umbrella at once.

CHAPTER TWENTY-ONE
SAVE THE WORLD

The entire field flashed green. Surprised screams started turning into angry growls. Then, there was another noise.

"Hmhmhmhahaha—" *Cough!* *Cough!* *Wheeeeeeze!* "HAHAHAHAHAHA!"

The astronaut singer's voice transformed from young pop star to cackling madman. It was Vincenzo himself!

"RUN!" Jackson yelled.

We started pushing through the mass of bodies, but getting out of the crowd was a lot harder than getting in. People had begun growing. They were getting scalier. In the sea of half-monsters, there was barely room to breathe, let alone move.

"YOU LIKE NEW ARMY?!" Vincenzo taunted over the speakers.

Jackson and I resorted to crawling between legs. I don't usually get nervous in tight spaces, but I was starting to feel super claustrophobic.

"NEW ARMY TAKE ISLAND!" Vincenzo continued. "NEW ARMY TAKE WORLD!"

Suddenly, I felt someone pick me up. One of the monsters must have taken offense to Jackson and me crawling between its legs because it lifted us above its head. That gave me a good view of the entire field. Oh man. It was 100 percent glowing green eyes. I looked down to see the monster open his jack-o-lantern mouth wide to swallow us whole. Welp. This was it. I closed my eyes and prepared for sharp teeth. Instead, I felt a bump.

What? I looked down to see our monster's neighbor shoving him. Apparently, our guy had accidentally thrown an elbow when he'd picked us up, and the other monster wasn't putting up with nonsense today. Our monster roared at him, then his buddy shoved harder. It was on now. Our monster threw Jackson, clenched his left fist, and punched his friend as hard as he could. Then he threw me and followed up that haymaker with a right hook.

I landed on my butt next to Jackson on the outskirts of the crowd. I scrambled to run away, but I didn't have to worry — nobody was paying attention to us. All of the glowing eyes were now focused on the fight in the middle of the field.

"Where's everyone else?" I asked.

Just then, Macy, Dale, and Mr. Pulawski joined us. "Are you guys OK?" Macy asked.

We couldn't answer over the growing commotion from the crowd. Other monsters had begun getting sucked into the fight, and the field was quickly devolving into chaos.

"STOP!" Vincenzo shouted so loud that every monster had to turn. Then, he pointed at us. "Get them."

For a second, nobody moved. Then, one monster in the front started charging. Not at us, but at Vincenzo.

"NO!" Vincenzo yelled. "THEM!"

The monster didn't listen. Neither did its buddies. Dozens of monsters rushed their creator and destroyed him. Then, they turned their attention to destroying the stage. Once they were done with the stage, I could only imagine what they'd do to the rest of the island. I turned to Macy and Jackson. They looked just as lost as I felt. If we hurried, maybe we could find a plane to escape before monsters destroyed the whole island, but that was the best we could do. Battle Island was beyond saving.

Then, Dale spoke up. "We need a stone."

Jackson motioned to the glowing, green umbrellas littering the field. "Take your pick."

"No, a purple one! We need to get their attention."

Mr. Pulawski suddenly broke into a big grin. "I like the way you think, mailman."

"Wait, why?" I asked. "What's that going to do?"

"And where are we going to find a purple umbrella?" Macy asked.

Suddenly, Jackson's eyes lit up. "The mayor!"

Of course! We'd left the mayor holding an umbrella! We all started sprinting back toward Jackson's house. Macy quickly took the lead, then I fell to the back of the pack with Mr. Pulawski. After a few seconds, even he pulled ahead of me. I thought that the 80-year-old was showing off, but then he turned and asked a question. "Do you still have those balloons?"

I dug through my pockets while I ran. To my surprise, I did still have the balloons. I handed them to Mr. Pulawski, and he split off in another direction. When we arrived at Jackson's house, we found the mayor sitting on the front steps, grinning like an idiot. "Is the concert over already?"

"Uh, yeah. Definitely over," Jackson gave him a weird look. "You didn't see what happened?"

"Yes!" the mayor answered defensively. Then he backtracked. "I mean, not all of it, you see, I, uh, had to go to the bathroom, and I was already in your house, so I took the liberty of..."

Jackson didn't have time for this story. He grabbed the umbrella. "I'll take this now!"

But the mayor wouldn't let it go. "Watch yourself, young man! You can't take things without asking!"

"You tried to give it to me earlier!"

"That was then, this is..."

SCREEEECH!

Just then, Mr. Pulawski pulled up on a rocket-powered ATV. "Mailman! Now!"

Dale pushed the mayor onto the back of the vehicle, and Mr. Pulawski peeled off. Macy, Jackson, and I stood there with our jaws on the ground for a second. "What did he do?" Macy finally asked.

"Check it out!" Dale responded.

Instead of chasing the ATV, Dale led us up a nearby hill. It turned out to be the perfect vantage point to see Mr. Pulawski's plan unfold. First, the old man zoomed around the monsters a few times. The screaming mayor and purple umbrella got their attention real fast. Then, he led them across the island to a tall oceanfront cliff. Finally, he gunned the engine and flew over the cliff.

WAAAAAAAAAHHHhhhhh!

The mayor's scream faded as he fell. Then —

SPLASH! SPLASH! SPLASH!

Each and every monster followed the ATV to their watery graves. Once the last monster disappeared, a colorful array of balloons rose above the cliff. Mr. Pulawski floated toward us looking exactly like the old guy from *Up*.

Dale and Macy cheered. "We did it!"

But Jackson and I knew better. Mr. Pulawski didn't save the island. At best, he'd only bought it a few minutes. I took a deep breath. We'd done this before, we could do it again. I turned to Dale. "Do you know any way we can rig the concert generator to zap all those umbrellas with electricity?"

"I'm sure I could figure it out, but..."

"Macy," I interrupted. "How many weapons do you have?"

"The monsters are gone."

"I asked how many weapons you have!"

"A lot."

"Get more." I turned to Jackson. "We need a wall."

"On it."

"Pete!" Macy grabbed my shoulder. "The monsters are gone. Why are you acting like this?!"

Just then, the ground started trembling. In seconds, the tremors grew so strong that they knocked us all to the ground. That's when Mr. Pulawski landed. "What's going on?"

"Killing the monsters doesn't turn them human or make them go away," Jackson explained. "It only makes them worse. Way worse!"

Mr. Pulawski looked at me. "Do we have a plan?"

I nodded. "But we need you on the team."

"I'll follow you kids anywhere."

BOOOOOOM!

We all looked toward the noise. It was Vincenzo's mountain. Or, more accurately, a pit where Vincenzo's mountain used to be. The sheer size of the monster army had caused the mountain to explode.

"ROOOOOAAAAAAAR!"

Gruesome monsters started clawing out of the hole, their glowing eyes locked on us.

I smiled at my team. "Let's go save the world."

A NOTE FROM THE AUTHOR

Thanks for reading my book! Hope you liked it. If you did, why not review it on Amazon? If you didn't, maybe keep it to yourself. You can also send me a message any time at matt@mattkorver.com.

49058684R00097

Made in the USA
Middletown, DE
17 June 2019